UNDER
PRESSURE
A DOSSIER NOVELLA

UNDER PRESSURE

A DOSSIER NOVELLA

CATHRYN FOX

Entangled Publishing, LLC
10940 S Parker Rd
Suite 327
Parker, CO 80134
rights@entangledpublishing.com

Scorched is an imprint of Entangled Publishing, LLC.

Edited by Candace Havens
Cover design by LJ Anderson
Cover art by OGphoto/Getty Images

Manufactured in the United States of America

First Edition September 2017

entangled
scorched

To Carolyn, Jodi, Valerie, and Sheila. I couldn't persuade any of you to go cage diving with me, but I sure had a lot of fun in Mexico with you ladies.

Chapter One

Reese

"I like the ocean, but come on. This is insane." As the high-tech, custom-built catamaran rocks beneath my feet, I glance at my best friend, Cole Rayburn. With his head cocked playfully, he grins at me like I'm some sort of chickenshit. I smack him in the gut, but when my hand lands on a solid pack of muscles, it hurts me more than him.

When had Cole gotten so freaking hard?

More importantly, why the hell am I noticing? This is my best friend we're talking about here. Yeah, okay, I haven't seen him shirtless in years, and he's always been solid. But now he's all muscle and power, deadly and fierce like one of the sharks circling our boat. Really, I shouldn't spend one more minute thinking about his hotness. A couple more seconds, sure, but definitely not a whole minute. That would just be wrong.

Saltwater splashes over me, and I push my damp hair from my forehead as I brace my legs. I glare at Cole. "Just because you're an adrenaline junkie who likes to live every day on the edge doesn't mean I'm not brave," I say and look at the galvanized shark cage—a floating structure the staff promises me is safe. I give an unladylike snort. They can assure me all they want. But I'm smart enough to know that once we're all crammed inside like sardines, we'll be dangling like bait.

I plant my hands on my hips and lift my chin. "I'm adventurous," I add. I'm not. At. All. "This just isn't my kind of adventure." Heading back to our gorgeous Cape Town hotel and soaking up the seaside sun—yeah, now that I could definitely get into.

Which makes me wonder why the adventure dossier I received from one of my friends—thanks to a New Year's Eve game we played—involved a trip to South Africa to go cage diving. With sharks. Big ones. Great white sharks, to be precise. Sure, I'm a veterinarian and love animals, but come on. I don't operate on anything that has thirty-five thousand teeth and can swallow me in one swift gulp.

Gulp...

"It's safe, Reesey Piecey," Cole says, and I glare at him for using the nickname he gave me when we were sixteen and I was stuffing my chubby face with a bag of sweet, candy-shelled chocolates. He was dating model-thin Jenny Garridy at the time. I used to call her the snake charmer. Then again, I had secret, hateful names for all his girlfriends, and believe me there were plenty of them. Weird that I can remember every last one and every freaking reason they were all wrong for Cole.

"Last I heard survival statistics were good. Not great, but good."

"Cole," I warn. Honest to God, we might be twenty-five now, but some things never change. Cole was always a kidder who liked to tease the hell out of me.

He laughs and drags me to him, the heat of his body doing the oddest things to me. Damn, maybe I shouldn't have taken those two extra seconds to think about his hotness.

"I'm kidding. It's one-hundred percent safe," he assures me.

"I hate you," I say. It's a lie. We've been best friends since I skinned my knee on the playground and he helped me home, but right now he's annoying me. And why doesn't he put on a damn shirt already?

"Hate you, too," he says, our usual endearment to each other when we mean the opposite. "You know I won't let anything happen to you," he says, his grin sliding into a concerned expression.

I give him a dubious look. Cole has always been there for me, but this isn't a breakup, a skinned knee, or my parents going through a nasty divorce. It's not the death of my sweet grandmother the night of the blackout during a wicked thunder and lightning storm, either. A shiver moves through me—the pets I care for at the clinic aren't the only ones afraid of bad weather.

This is me, not-so-brave Reese Scott, jumping into the water with a handful of hungry sharks, and last time I checked, Cole was a lot of things, but a shark-fighter was not one of them. Which begs the question, why is he on this trip with me, anyway? Yeah, he's an athlete who runs wilderness tours in Colorado, and he's a level-six white water rafting guide, but this trip is supposed to be all about celebrating the second half of my twenties in an epic way—that is, finding a hot guy and having back-bending sex before returning home. How the heck can that happen with Cole hanging around? Not that I really plan on having sex with anyone. After getting dumped by my fiancé, I am so over men. Seriously, he thought I was trying to turn him into something he wasn't? When did wanting to add a little fun and spontaneity to the relationship become me trying to change him? Jerk.

Cole, while he might be the epitome of fun and spontaneity, shouldn't be here with me. I can stand on my own two feet without him hovering over me all the time, thank you very much. I have been doing it since he left New York to work in Colorado a year ago, right after I got engaged. He only returned home last month, temporarily leaving a job he loves to work with his uncle in construction to make ends meet while visiting—or rather, while keeping a close eye on me. But I can't think about that right now because the captain is waving me over. Apparently, it's my turn to jump to my death.

Even though my insides are in chaos, I try to appear calm, and take soothing breaths, in through the nose and out through the mouth.

"Hey," Cole says, and when I turn back to him, he's standing over me, rubbing his knuckles over my arm in a comforting manner. Presenting composure—even though this is Cole, and nothing gets by him when it comes to me—I lift my chin to meet his gaze. When he turns those ocean-blue eyes on me, as deep and complex as the Atlantic waters crashing against the side of the vessel, I feel a measure of calm. Cole really is a good guy, a great catch. Why the hell isn't he taken already?

Because he's an adventure seeker and has no desire to get serious or put down roots.

Oh, right.

Cole dips his head, and those kissable lips of his are right there, near my mouth. If I wanted to kiss him all I'd have to do is go up on my tiptoes. But I don't want to kiss him. This is my best friend. I'm not sure why I suddenly need to keep reminding myself of that.

Get yourself together, girl.

"You're in good hands. I promise," he says as he continues to run his knuckles along my arm. Oh, he has good hands, all right. A shiver races down my spine.

What the hell? He's touched me a million times and I've never gotten all tingly before—and what the hell is going on with my nipples? Seriously, enough already! Must be nerves from this adventure. Has to be. It's the only logical explanation. Then again, it could be because I haven't had sex in, like, forever.

"Come on—we need to suit up." Cole holds my shoulders and turns me toward the back of the boat, where the crew and wetsuits await. He follows me closely, the warmth of his body chasing back the cold in mine. I stare into the water as I get sized for a wetsuit, boots, and hoodie. Cole and I both climb into the gear and listen to the instructions as we, and six other thrill-seekers step into the cage.

I rest my feet on the platform and move closer to Cole. He smiles at me and adjusts my eye goggles. The crew slowly lowers the cage into the water, the big white flotation devices attached to it keeping it buoyant. Our heads remain above surface, and I don't have to hold my breath and dip under if I don't want to, but I've come too far to back down. Plus, if I chicken out now, it will only give Cole ammunition, and he's teased me enough for one day—in far too many ways. From the boat, the guide fills a rubber seal-shaped decoy with chum, and my stomach sort of turns. Great, any second now I'm going to lose two things: my lunch and my dignity.

Cole nudges me and points down. I submerge to see a big freaking shark, with big freaking teeth clamping onto the side of the cage. I panic, and I'm about ready to scramble back onto the boat when Cole wraps his arms around me and pushes upward until we burst through the surface.

"Oh my God," I shriek.

"Pretty cool, right?"

"Cool?" Was he serious? "That scared the crap out of me."

"Yeah, but now you know you're safe. They can't get in. Come on, let's go back under."

I mull that over for a quick second. I guess it was kind of

cool, and the shark couldn't get near me. I look at the structure surrounding me and feel a little more confident.

"Okay." I suck in another breath and go under with Cole. He keeps his arm around me, and I slide mine around him to keep him close.

More sharks come, and while it is scary, it is kind of exciting, too. A shark hits the cage and it jolts me, but Cole is right there holding tight—protecting and helping me out—like always. I steal a glance and find him looking at me, not the set of teeth trying to get at us. He smiles, and it's weird how my heart seems to skip a beat. I probably never would have climbed into this cage if it weren't for him. Maybe I do need him more than I let on. Maybe that's why the friend who drew my name sent Cole along—so I'd go through with it.

The truth is, I missed him so much when he left New York. His departure ripped my heart in two, but who was I to hold him back? Yeah, we were close, the tightest of friends, but I was engaged and he needed to find himself, live his own life.

Cole looks away, but before he does, I catch something in his eyes. Something that just might resemble...*desire*. My pulse jumps a notch and my entire body tightens. Confusing feelings surface, and I can't believe how girly I am in my reaction to him.

You are a girl.

Not to Cole, though.

Surely I'm mistaken. Must be the water on my goggles, obscuring my vision and making me see things that aren't there. Cole doesn't think of me as anything other than the pig-tailed tomboy next door. And I don't think of him as anything other than the scrawny boy who lived beside me—one who always protected me, helped me with everything, and grew into a smoking hot guy with a killer body that I suddenly can't seem to keep my eyes—or hands—off of.

Oh shit.

Chapter Two

COLE

I stretch out on the catamaran, and I can't help but smile at Reese as she bites into her chicken wrap and chews like she hasn't had a meal in days. "Cage diving really builds up an appetite, huh?"

She nods, and her big brown eyes go wide. "That was actually kind of fun."

"Want to do it again tomorrow?" I ask.

Her hand stills just as she's about to take another bite. She lifts her head, but her act of bravado isn't fooling me. "I would, but we're hitting the Spookdraai hiking trail tomorrow. Then the day after we have that African wildlife tour and game drive safari. All part of my dossier, remember?"

I laugh and nudge her chin with my fist. "I remember. You were brave today, Reesey Piecey." I gave her that nickname when we were kids, partly because her name is Reese and partly because she is as sweet as those little chocolate candies she's always popping into her mouth.

"I'm brave every day," she counters, then chews her sandwich. She swallows and adds, "I just don't know why one of my friends would put me in a dangerous situation where I had to prove it. I mean, I like animals and all, but still."

My gaze moves over her face as she takes a drink and continues to talk about this adventure she's on. My stomach tightens as I listen. She always tries to present a brave face, but she doesn't have to pretend anything with me. I know her better than she knows herself, and she's been through a lot over the last few years, which makes me feel like a total and utter prick for taking off to Colorado. But fuck, how could I have stayed in New York? Watching her with that asshole Jared nearly fucking killed me. Every time he touched her, kissed her, walked into a room with her, it was all I could do not to punch him in the face. I never liked the guy. Then again, I never liked any guy she dated.

How could I, when I had a secret crush on her for years? But no way am I about to jeopardize our friendship by telling her. She thinks of me only as a friend, and I couldn't risk losing her by spilling my guts. Besides that, I'm not the guy for her. She's the white picket fence and family kind of girl, where I'm an adrenaline junkie out for the next adventure. There hasn't been a guy in my family who could settle down, not even my father. Bastard left when we were just kids.

I toss the last of my wrap into my mouth and take a long pull from my water bottle. I shift and rest my back against the catamaran as we head back to shore. Around us, the others are taking their lunch to the back of the vessel to watch the video of the dive, but I'd rather hang out and enjoy the sunshine for a bit longer with Reese. I missed her so goddamn much when I was away.

"I want to hear me more about this pact you made with your friends," I say. She's told me bits and pieces, but I get the feeling she's still holding information from me, which is weird because she tells me everything. Or at least she used to.

"What do you want to know?"

I lean into her, and when my leg touches hers, she flinches. The movement is slight, but I still notice it, even when others might not have. Okay, what the hell was that all about? When did she ever not want me to touch her? Shit, I hope she didn't see the way I was looking at her earlier. Usually I can keep my shit together, but seeing her big eyes, wide and excited beneath the mask, looking so adorable as she faced a shark, fucked me over big time. All I wanted to do was pull her against me and kiss the hell out of her.

I clear my throat. "Well, Olivia ended up staying in Italy with Gio, and Kennedy hooked up with Sean in London and now the two are living together in Chicago. Are you all on a marriage quest or something?"

"Not…exactly," she says and crinkles her nose.

"Then what exactly?"

She shrugs like it's nothing, which makes me realize it *is* something. Now I want to know all the more.

"It's silly," she says.

"Tell me."

She huffs. "You're not going to let this go, are you?"

"No."

She throws one hand up in surrender. "Fine, we're supposed to find a man and have epic sex. Those two girls had deeper feelings for the men they chose to have sex with — heck, they were already in love, which is why they're still together after the adventure."

My stomach punches into my throat. "You've got to be fucking kidding me. Whose idea was this, anyway? Harper's?" She always was the wild one in the group. She'd hit on me a few times, but I wasn't interested. Sure, I fooled around. A lot. But that was only to try to keep my mind off Reece. Didn't fucking work.

She nods. "Yeah, but we all agreed to it."

I give a hard shake of my head, and my damp hair falls into my eyes. I shove it back. "No way are you having sex with some stranger, Reese." Her gaze jerks to mine and she gives me a strange look. Shit. "You're in a foreign country and it's dangerous," I add, to cover how I really feel.

"You're right," she says, a look of sadness on her face as she stares off into the distance. "I'm not."

My stomach squeezes. Christ, I really need to beat the hell out of Jared for hurting her.

"Good," I say. Tension eases from my shoulders to know she's not going to do something dangerous. Christ, if she wants epic sex, I can give her that.

Wait! What?

"And it's not because it's dangerous. It's because I'm off men. Done with relationships."

I don't know whether to laugh or cry. I can't stomach the thought of her with another man, but if she's off men, done with relationships, then she'll never be mine.

She'll never be yours, anyway, asshole. She doesn't like you like that, and you're not the guy for her.

Still, Jared is definitely getting a beatdown when I get home. He'd hurt her so badly she no longer believes in true love and happily ever after. Fucker. Even if I were going to make a move on her, offer her epic sex, which I'm clearly not going to, I couldn't do it now, anyway. Not when she's hurting and still upset over the breakup.

Wanting to lighten her mood, I say, "Well, if you're off men, at least you're in the right profession."

"What do you mean? How does being a veterinarian help me?"

"You don't have to go far to start collecting cats." She whacks me, but it does bring a smile to her face. Then, at the same time, we say, "Mrs. Jones."

I shake my head. "That woman was bat-shit crazy." Christ, when we were kids, we all used to take the long way to the playground to avoid her house at the end of the street.

Reese smacks her palm to her forehead. "God, I'm going to turn out just like Mrs. Jones, aren't I?"

I nudge her. "Don't worry. I won't let that happen to you." As the vessel reaches the pier, I grab our wrappers and package everything back in the box we were given. "I'm going to buy a video. Maybe we can watch it tonight."

She nods and I reach for her hand to help her up. The boat sways, and her body collides with mine. I wrap my hand around her and feel the warmth of her skin beneath my fingertips. Fuck, she feels good. My cock thickens as her breasts push against my chest. She is so fucking perfect.

Her hands go around my back, and I become hyperaware that her tiny little bikini and my swim shorts are the only things separating us. What I wouldn't do to feel skin on skin, to taste my way from her mouth to the spot between her legs. As my mind conjures the route my tongue will take, I harden even more. A strange, strangled sound catches in Reese's throat, and I want to inch back and apologize. *Would* inch back and apologize, if I had any fucking blood left in my damn brain.

"Cole," she squeaks, and the sound snaps me back to reality.

Back the fuck off, dude.

"Uh, yeah," I say, but as I step away, I don't miss the way her hands linger on my body, or the way her gaze dips to see me in all my hard glory. She stares for a moment, a pink flush crawling up her cheeks. Her lips part, and her chest rises and falls as her gaze lingers. *She's fucking checking me out.* The girl I've been crushing on since I was eight is checking me out.

I stand there and let her, but she can't for one minute think she's going to get an eyeful and I'm not. I take in those sweet, lush lips I want to suck on. My gaze drops to her breasts, a little smaller now that she lost so much weight. They'd fit into my mouth so nicely. I take in her tanned skin, the soft curves of her hips, and those long legs I'd cut off my left nut to feel wrapped around my back.

I slide my gaze back up, and when my eyes lock on hers, see the heat reflected there, I want to drop to my hands and knees and howl at the damn moon.

"Right this way, everyone," one of the crewmembers says, pulling me back from my fantasy—one that has been plaguing my dreams for years.

"We, ah...we should go," I say, my voice an octave lower.

"Yeah. It's a long drive back to the hotel."

"Let me get that video, okay?"

Needing a reprieve so I don't take her right here on the catamaran and ruin everything between us, I turn and leave her standing there. But when I feel her eyes drilling into me, I look over my shoulder and catch the way she's staring at my ass. Son of a bitch. She's still checking me out.

So, what am I going to do about that?

Chapter Three

Honest to God, I have no idea what the hell happened between Cole and me on the boat yesterday—okay, maybe I have *some* idea—but were we seriously checking each other out? Gazing at each other with pure lust in our eyes? We're *best friends,* for God's sake. Best friends don't look at each other like that, right?

Must be the tropical air.

From beneath the wide brim of my sun hat, I steal a glance at him as we hike along the cliffs of Spookdraai Mountain, a trail that is supposed to be haunted with discontented souls who wander up and down the coastline. Cole looks my way, but I'm far too slow to react. His eyes turn a deeper shade of blue when he catches me staring, and his gaze drops to my parted lips. Feeling breathless beneath his intense stare, I suck in air, but can't seem to refill my damn lungs.

"Doing okay?" he asks.

I nod as he checks in with me. "Yeah, I guess I need to hit

the treadmill more often," I say to cover the real reason I can't seem to breathe. What the hell is going on between us?

"You're perfect," he says. I've heard him say that to me before, even before I lost the excess weight, but why does it suddenly sound more sexual, more suggestive?

Because you two were checking each other out, and he had a huge freaking hard-on.

Oh, right.

"This is just a tough climb for someone who's not used to it." He stops and looks over the cliff. I follow his gaze and the water is so clear that I can see numerous shipwrecked boats on the ocean floor. The scenery around us is magnificent, breathtaking really, but my eyes keep coming back to Cole.

Dammit. Dammit. Dammit.

He shrugs off his backpack and adjusts his ball cap, shoving his bangs inside. "We've been traveling for over an hour now. Let's take a break, get a drink, and have something to eat." He gestures with a nod to the little ghost sign up ahead. "There's a small cave over there where we can get out of the sun."

"I'm not going into any cave," I shoot back quickly.

His gaze darts to mine, a small grin playing on his mouth, making him look boyishly handsome. Except after yesterday, seeing him shirtless and feeling his arousal, I know there is nothing boyish about him. "Why not?"

I plant one hand on my hip and glare at the cave. "Some girl who survived a shipwreck and made it up to one of the caves where she died, haunts them, remember."

"Come on. You don't believe in all that, do you?"

I step closer to the cliff and point to the water. "Of course, I do. Look at all those sunken boats. There are a lot of lost souls up here. And you read the sign back there. It says hikers can hear her singing in the caves sometimes."

His grin widens. "Don't worry. I won't—"

I cut him off. "I know. I know. You won't let anything happen to me. You're even going to protect me from becoming a crazy cat lady." How he's going to do that is beyond me.

I follow him and watch his broad muscles shift under his T-shirt. He steps into the cave, and I nearly crash into him when he comes to an abrupt halt. "Shh, hear that?" he asks.

"Oh my God, Cole." I practically crawl up his back. "Is it singing? Tell me it's not singing," I say, my voice bordering on hysteria.

Cole laughs, and the sound echoes in the cave as he slides his hands around his back to hold me. "No, it's not singing. It's silence. We're the only ones here, Reesey Piecey. Relax."

"I hate you," I say, then pinch his side for teasing me, although what I really want is to pinch his ass, thanks to the way it looks so cute in his shorts. "You scared me half to death."

He flinches. "Hate you, too. Now come on, let's get some food. I'm starving."

"You're always starving." I curl his shirt in my hands and follow him. I tug when he goes too deep. "Let's stay close to the mouth of the cave, just in case."

With light pouring in, I let him go, find a flat spot, and sit crossed leg on the cool ground, a nice reprieve from the heat outside. Cole moves in beside me and I ditch my hat. When he looks at me, I run my fingers through my hat hair and try to fix it. The man has seen me at my worst. Cripes, he'd even held my hair back the night I turned sixteen and thought it would be a good idea to drink a few shots of Patron. So I have no idea why I'm suddenly trying to make myself presentable.

Because you want his damn body.

Oh, right.

As that shocked realization settles in my passion-rattled brain, I open the backpack and pull out our sandwiches, compliments of our hotel. Cole takes a long pull from his water bottle and hands it to me. We've drunk from the same bottles since we were kids, swapped a ton load of spit, yet it never felt intimate before, like it does right now. I take a drink and recap it.

Cole repositions himself until his back is against the rock wall. "Come here," he says, and I shuffle until I'm beside him, our thighs touching. Hyperaware of everything Cole — his breath, his body, his every movement — I bite into my sandwich and try to push the bread down my tight throat.

"We have the safari tomorrow," I say as sexual tension fills the small cave.

"Yeah, I know." Why does his voice sound so much deeper? Oh, probably because he must feel this sexual shift between us, too.

Cole's hand lands on my bare thigh, his thumb sweeping back and forth, brushing my tingling skin. Does he even know he's doing that? I'm not sure he does, but the hungry spot between my legs is well aware what his innocent touch is doing to my body. Odd really, considering he's caressed me like this numerous times before — a friendly, caring touch — and it never melted my bones the way it does now.

"Why do you think my friends keep putting me in dangerous situations?"

"I don't know," he says. "They all know you're a chickenshit, so I'm not really sure."

"I'm not a chickenshit," I counter, and whack his stomach.

Big mistake.

He grabs my hand and holds it to his body. Unable to help myself, I rub the back of my knuckles over his six-pack. God, he is so hard and yummy. I bite the inside of my cheek to stop from moaning. A growl rumbles in Cole's throat, and I steal a quick glance at him in time to catch the tortured look crossing his face.

Holy hell!

I shake my head, hardly able to believe Cole Rayburn, my best friend, is groaning as I touch him. What the ever-loving fuck is going on between us? A flapping noise comes from somewhere deep in the cave, and my heart leaps.

"Cole," I say, and practically scurry into his lap. "What was that?"

"Probably just a bird," he mumbles. "Don't worry. I've got you."

His arm goes around me, and he's rubbing my side, a long slow sweep, that brushes along my outer breast. My nipples tighten painfully, begging for his hand, his mouth. His head turns, and with enough light shining in through the mouth of the cave, I can see the turbulence in his eyes. His jaw clenches and he turns away. His breathing has changed, become more erratic.

"Cole?"

He scrubs his chin and exhales sharply, less composed than I've ever seen him. "Yeah."

Trembling with a need so foreign to me, I lean into him, even though every instinct I possess is screaming in warning.

"You okay?" I ask, positive neither of us is currently in our right minds. Must be something in the air. Has to be. We've never acted like this around each other before.

"I don't think so," he says as heat simmers between us. The cave is suddenly so hot I can't breathe.

He turns my way, shifts his body until we're both sitting crossed-legged facing each other. His hand goes to my cheek, a soft touch as he slides his big palm around my neck.

"Reese," he whispers, but before I can say anything, he dips his head and his lips close over mine, warm and soft, yet hungry and demanding. His tongue slides into my mouth, and when it finds mine, it steals the last of my breath and all of my common sense. A moan I have no control over crawls from my throat, and he deepens the kiss—hot and firm, taking full control. I've kissed Cole before, but never, ever like this.

He drags me onto his lap and his cock—a rock-hard cock, thank you very much—presses against my ass as I let my legs fall over his outer thighs. My knees hit the ground as I straddle him and shamelessly gyrate on his lap. I'm acting like some desperate girl who hasn't had sex in ages, a girl who would—and is—jumping on the first man to present her with a hard-on. But I don't care because it's true. I am a desperate girl, and I need this.

His fingers tighten on my hips and when he powers upward, I move with him, hardly able to believe I'm dry-humping my best friend in the middle of a goddamn haunted cave. We shouldn't be doing this. We shouldn't be doing this.

"We shouldn't be doing this."

"I know," he says. "We shouldn't."

Shit, did I say that out loud? *Shut your damn mouth, Reese. You know you want this, even if it's wrong.*

His hand slides to my shoulders and presses down, grinding his cock harder against me. He moans into my mouth, his tongue brushing over my bottom lip, tasting me, savoring me. I grip his hair, swiftly run my fingers through it, wanting to touch every inch of him before we both come to our senses. I can't understand this pull between us, this need clawing at my insides, demanding to be sated. Is it the same for him? I have little time to think about that as warm heat floods me, and I swear to God if he doesn't strip me naked and touch every inch of me in the next five minutes, I might just die. Then I'll be the one haunting the damn cave forever.

"Cole," I whisper, a desperate sort of ache in my voice.

He breaks the kiss and when he pulls back, we're both left breathless. Guilt flashes in his eyes. "Fuck, you're right. Sorry."

I shake my head because he's mistaken the desperation he's heard. It wasn't for him to stop. It was for him to continue. But this is wrong and we shouldn't be doing it. But why, oh why, does it feel so right?

"Cole," I say again, my lust-buzzed mind trying to string a sentence together.

"Yeah."

"Why…why did you kiss me?" I ask, not only because I need to say something, but because, deep inside, I'm curious about this sudden need we're displaying.

His gaze moves over my face, a careful assessment. He must see the want in my eyes because his expression changes from apologetic to hungry. "I was helping you out," he whispers, his voice playful as he brushes his thumb over my cheek, the intimacy in his touch going right through me.

"Helping me out?" I ask, playing along, desperately wanting to see where this leads. "With what?" Not that I care. I just like this intimate conversation, the way his warm breath is washing over my face as we talk, not to mention the way his big hands are touching me with such soft recognition, tugging my shirt out from my shorts.

"A list of things, really," he murmurs.

"Oh, okay." A moment of silence and then, "Will it require more kissing?"

He brushes my hair from my shoulder. His fingers burn over my quivering flesh. "Yeah, but that's not all it will require."

"No."

"No, I'm going to have to do things to you, Reese. Dirty things."

Oh. My. God. I'm seriously dying here. Cole is going to do dirty things to me! I shouldn't be this happy. I really shouldn't. This could be so bad for our friendship. But, holy hell, the heat between my legs is telling me not to think too hard on that right now. Not when there are other *hard* things I should be thinking about.

"What…what kind of dirty things?" I ask, loving the

direction this is going, despite my best interests.

"I'm going to take these clothes off you and kiss every inch of your body."

Alrighty, then. I didn't see that coming, but I always did love the man's spontaneity.

"Okay."

Okay? That's all I can come up with? Then again, how can I possibly counter with a witty comeback? My body is on fire, burning up, under terrible pressure. If he doesn't touch me soon, I'm afraid something might blow.

Blow.

Oh God, why did that word pop into my rattled brain? Probably because I can't stop thinking about his cock, the long length of it, the hardness, and the way it pressed against me on the boat—the way it's pressing against my ass right freaking now. I should not be lusting after my best friend. If I knew what was good for me, I'd tap out right now and shove this crazy need so far back in my mind that it never sees the light again.

Walk away, girl. Just walk away.

I blink up at him innocently and continue to play along. "Then what?"

So much for doing what's good for me.

"Then I'm going to put my cock inside you."

I quiver at his bluntness. I've never heard Cole talk like this before—playful *and* sexy—and I can't deny that it's damn exciting.

"How is that helping me out?" I ask.

Cole is going to put his cock in me, and I need to stop asking questions already!

Another eerie noise jostles me back to the present, and I turn. "What was that?" I whisper. "Was it singing?" Could the cave be haunted?

He tears off his T-shirt, tosses it behind me, and bends

forward until I'm flat out underneath him. He shifts his weight and slides his hand between my legs. "The only singing we're going to hear is when I strum your body right here, and you're calling out my name in orgasm."

OMFG, if that's isn't music to my ears, I don't know what is.

His lips close over mine again, taking full possession, and I writhe beneath his invading tongue, hungry for everything he's going to do to me. I run my hands over his bare back, and when I palm his muscles, they bunch beneath my fingers. He is so hard and solid it's insane. I take a breath and try to control myself, but I can't, so instead I lightly drag my nails over his flesh as his mouth goes to the sensitive spot on my neck.

The air around us is heavy with sexual energy, and I'm pretty sure we're giving off enough sparks to light up the damn cave. I hear another shuffling noise and crane my neck to see outside.

"Cole," I whispered. "What if someone comes?"

His soft chuckle vibrates through me. "Oh, don't worry, someone's going to come."

My body is quivering and I don't want him to stop, but smack him anyway. "I'm serious."

He moans against my neck. "I am, too."

"I hate you," I say.

"I hate you, too." His wet tongue sweeps over my flesh then he puts a hand on either side of my head and pushes up. "But while we're here on vacation, I'm still going to help you out."

"With what?" I ask for the millionth time.

"You don't want to be like Mrs. Jones, right?"

"No, you're right. I don't."

"So, by having sex, I'm helping you from becoming a crazy cat lady."

I do like his way of thinking. But what will this do to us? I don't want to lose him because some sort of tropical lust bug has bitten us this weekend.

"And you know, since you're here on this adventure for epic sex, and I don't happen to have any plans, we're killing all kinds of birds with one stone."

One stone? Oh yes, one very big, very hard stone pressing against my leg.

"So, you're keeping me from becoming a crazy cat lady and helping me fulfill my adventure."

"Yeah, what a guy, huh?"

I laugh. "I'll say."

"The things I'd do for you, Reese."

"You're a very good friend, Cole."

"The best," he says, his eyes glinting playfully.

"And after the vacation?"

"Things go back to normal. You and me, best friends."

God, could I really do that?

Then again, could I really not do this?

He lifts my T-shirt, his gaze moving over my body like it's the first time he's seen it. "Sit up," he whispers, all humor gone from his face.

I inch up until my mouth is near his nipple, and as he slides his hand around my back to release my bra clasp with practiced ease, I flick my tongue out and lick him, reveling in the warm, salty taste of his skin.

He flinches. "Jesus." I do it again, and he growls. "Arms up." I lift, and he peels off my T-shirt and removes my bra. "Lie back down."

I catch the heat in his eyes as he makes me a small pillow with my shirt and his, tucking them carefully under my head. We might have just agreed to sex, but my heart tightens at the way he's making me comfortable first and foremost. I've missed him since he left New York. A lot. Too much.

With a touch so gentle I could weep, he lightly strokes my

breasts, his thumbs caressing my nipples. Does he touch all his lovers like this? If so, no wonder women are clamoring for a second time with him. But he has a revolving door, and a rule about never the same woman twice. Seriously, though, after experiencing his brand of lovemaking, who in their right mind would want any other man touching their body.

Lovemaking? What the hell?

It's sex, Reese.

"These…" His soft breath washes over my quivering nipples as he zeroes in on them. "I have so many ideas for what I'm going to do to these." He bends and swipes the soft blade of his tongue over one nipple.

"Cole," I croak.

His gaze moves to mine, and his playfulness is back. "What's wrong? Still afraid someone might come?"

"Yeah," I say, so turned on it's hard to think straight. The walls of the cave close in on me, nothing in the world existing but this man and the things he's promising me.

"What about the ghost? Still afraid this place is haunted?" I nod and wonder what kind of game he's playing. "Don't you see? I'm helping you out with that, too."

"How could you possibly help with that?" I ask.

"By making you moan loud enough to scare it away."

Yes, please.

"That's very good thinking, Cole."

"I do what I can," he says, and this time he pulls that same hard nipple into his mouth. I arch my back and whimper.

"Oh, so good…" I run my nails over his back, and when he growls, it thrills me that he's as into this as I am.

Pressure builds between my legs, and I widen them. His cock presses against the hungry spot needing his touch, and I lift slightly, moving against him.

He softens his tongue and leisurely glides it over my other nipple and I whimper louder. "That's it, Reese. Keep making noises like that." He bites down, sucks my nub between his teeth.

"Yes," I cry out and grip his hair to keep his mouth on me.

His soft chuckle vibrates through my body, and my nipples tighten even more. I moan and toss my head, my hair tangling beneath me. His mouth leaves my breasts and I cry out at the loss, but when he goes lower, my yelp of disappointment turns into a cry of approval. His tongue burns my flesh as he licks a path to the button on my shorts, and I gasp when he rips into them with his teeth.

"I think I need to find other ways to make you moan," he teases. "But don't worry. I have a lot of ideas."

Thank you, universe.

Once he has the button open, he grips my shorts and slowly slides them down my legs, leaving my thong in place. My God, I could climax just from the way he's looking at my barely there panties. I'm sure many women have seen that look in Cole's eye before, but until today, I've never been lucky enough.

"You still with me, Reese?" he asks, since I've gone quiet.

I can take care of myself, but truthfully, I kind of like the way he always checks in with me. "Yes," I say, my hands going to my breasts.

His nostrils flare as his hands grip my thighs and widen them. He tugs the string on my thong, runs his finger along it, and pushes it to the side to completely expose my sex. Admiration fills his face and does the strangest things to me. "Yeah, when I'm through, your throat is going to be raw from all the screaming I'm going to make you do."

I love a confident man.

Heat suffuses my body, as he leans in and fills his lungs with my aroused scent. My body hums with tension, a desperate sort of ache taking hold as he wets his bottom lip like he's preparing for a feast.

"Please…" I whimper.

He looks at me, his features taut with hunger, and it arouses me even more. "Yeah, keep talking to me, Reese." I tremble from his gaze, his words, as he runs his thumb over my nether lips, widening my sex, and lightly nudging my swollen clit. I revel in the needy way he's touching me, the possessive way he takes in my nakedness. "Keep scaring the ghost away."

With one quick tug, he tears my panties from my hips, and I gasp out loud. He grins, and tucks them into his back pocket like they're some sort of souvenir. "I'll replace them," he murmurs and then flattens himself on the ground and slides his hands under my ass to lift my body to his mouth.

The first sweet touch of his tongue to my clit sends sparks shooting through me, and stars dance on the cave walls. The temperature in the cave skyrockets, and my body grows hot, too hot. His tongue slides and caresses as he eats at me, and his loud moans are matching mine. I'm not sure who is turned on more here. He pushes his tongue inside, and I clench around him. Tremors begin in my core, and Cole growls louder.

A shuddery little breath escapes my lungs as he sucks, nibbles, and pushes a finger inside me. I writhe shamelessly and reach for him as he fills me. His tongue slicks and curls over me, back and forth, back and forth, a torturous tease, and volcanic pressure builds. I try to breathe past it. I am so not ready for this to end.

The truth is, I've had sex before, but what this man is doing to me is blowing my damn mind. But maybe that's it. Maybe it's different because I'm with my best friend, a guy who truly cares about me, and vice versa.

"That's it," he whispers against my clit, the vibration bringing on a rush of wetness. His fingers burrow deep, and I draw in a sharp breath as the world closes in on me. Completely lost in the moment—in Cole—I shut my eyes. Drugged, already addicted, I give in to everything pulling at me. I move restlessly as my sex pulses and I tumble into an intense orgasm.

"Cole," I cry out as I shatter around his fingers.

"Keep coming for me, Reece," he responds from between my legs, the need in his voice spiking my desire as he laps at me, drinking in all my liquid desire.

I shake beneath him as he buries his face in my sex. He stays between my thighs for a long time, lapping and licking until he's had his fill. A fluttering noise reaches my ears, and when he finally lifts his head and I see moisture around his mouth—my hot desire wetting his face—it arouses me all over again. His grin is wicked, sexy, and my breath catches at the playful way he's looking at me.

"Hear that?" he asks.

I listen, and I hear something flutter. "Yeah."

"You weren't loud enough. I need to rectify that."

He pushes to his feet to rip into his pants. I scurry backward a bit when he releases his cock, so big and hard for me that I nearly swallow my tongue.

His head dips, the muscles along his jaw clenching. "You okay, Reese?" he asks as he takes his cock into his hand and strokes it.

"Yeah," I manage, but I can't tear my gaze away as he rubs himself, long steady pumps that make me ache to feel him inside me.

He snatches the water bottle, opens it, and presses it to my mouth. "Drink."

I take a long pull, then he finishes what's left and shoves it into his backpack. I swipe my tongue over my bottom lip, wetting my dry skin.

Cole groans, a deep, tortured sound, so sexy and needy it gives me an idea. A dirty, delicious, naughty idea. He likes to play during sex, but two can enjoy his game, right? "You know," I begin and point at him, "your voice is much deeper than mine. If you ask me, I think your moans might be just what we need to scare the ghost away."

His eyes narrow, but before he can say anything, I go up on my knees and take his hard cock into my hungry mouth.

"Holy fuuuuck," he growls, and the sound echoes around us, proving my point. "That is so hot."

I draw what I can of him to the back of my throat, and he gently grips my hair. His moans grow louder, but I can hardly hear them through the thundering of my heart. I lick his pre-cum and suck harder, working for more. His muscles are so tight, his blood flowing so fast, I know he's close. While I want to taste him, selfish girl that I am, I'm too desperate to have him inside me to let him come in my mouth. But there'll be time for that later. We still have plenty of vacation left.

Wait, this should probably be a one-time-only thing, right? I should clarify that.

He tugs on my hair. "Reese, you need to stop."

I inch back and wipe my mouth with the back of my hand. "Why?" I ask innocently, and he just growls at me.

"On your back. It's time for me to fuck you."

I fall onto the makeshift pillow and stare up at his magnificent body, all hard lines and grooves I can't wait to explore with my hands and tongue. He drops to his knees, and I widen my thighs to accommodate him.

He leans into me and that's when it occurs to me that we need protection. I can't freaking believe I nearly forgot. But my body is on sensory overload, so far gone that it's like I'm having an out-of-body experience, and that's messing with me in dangerous ways.

"Condom," I say, my voice cracking.

Cole fists his hair. "Shit, right. Sorry about that."

"You have one?"

Please let him have one!

"Yeah," he says and grabs his shorts.

Cripes, I don't know what I was worried about. This is Cole. An adrenaline-junkie adventure guide who is always prepared for everything.

If only I were prepared for this.

He grabs a condom. "I can't believe I almost forgot," he says, his deep voice rippling through me as he quickly sheathes himself then settles between my legs. I guess this sex is messing with him as much as it is me.

"Ready to scream, Reesey Piecey?"

I grin. Honestly, I never knew sex could be so much fun. "Yes," I murmur against his throat.

He rubs his cock up to caress my clit, teasing the ever-living hell out of me. If his goal is to make me scream from want, then he's seriously headed down the right road. His crown circles my hard nub languidly, and my entire body tingles in anticipation.

With single-minded determination, I move, lift, and shift, anything to force him inside, but he clearly has other plans, and I believe they involve driving me out of my mind. I fear I'm going to start babbling like an idiot soon. That would for sure scare any ghosts away.

His crown circles, teases, and slips in an inch, only to withdraw. Pressure builds in my body as desperation takes hold.

Enough already.

I pinch his back and he chuckles. "What's the matter, Reesey Piecey?"

"You know what's the matter."

"Sorry, you're going to have to tell me."

"Hate you," I say.

"Hate you, too."

His tip enters, giving me only an inch, and a cry lodges in my throat, his teasing becoming too much. I need him. Now.

"Cole, please," I beg.

"Keep talking to me, Reese. Keep making lots of noise," he says, acting like he has all the patience in the world, but I can sense his restraint, his fight for control. He's as desperate to be inside me as I am to have him. But for some reason he's holding himself back.

"I need your cock," I say, and don't care if I sound like an eager nymphomaniac because right now, there is no better way to describe me.

He shoves a little deeper inside, and when he gives a husky groan, my eyes roll in my head. My sex clenches, and it's almost scary how much I want this—how much I need him.

"Is this what you want? Is this what's going to make you moan louder?"

"Yes," I say. "This is exactly what I need."

His sharp intake of breath doesn't go unnoticed by me as I fall back onto the makeshift pillow. He powers forward and fills me even more, and I don't care who the hell is in the vicinity. I let go of all inhibitions and just whimper without care.

"Good, so damn good," I say, and grip him with my sex muscles to keep him from pulling out again.

"Fuck, yes," he says, and rewards me by burying himself deep. "I can't wait for you to come around my cock," he whispers in my ear.

I give a broken gasp as his words echo through me. "Yes. Fuck me, Cole. Hard," I cry out as he fills me in a way I've never been filled before. My muscles suck him in, and I clench around him, but he pulls out, and the sweet friction nearly sends me soaring to the moon. His mouth finds mine again, and he fills me even more as his veins become engorged with heated blood.

His chest pushes against mine, rubbing and stimulating my aching nipples as he moves over me. He presses harder, strokes faster, and every nerve in my body is screaming as the need builds, reaching a point of no return. We move together, finding a natural rhythm like we've been doing this our entire lives. I must say, we've done a lot of things together, but sadly, this wasn't one of them. I'm so glad we're rectifying that.

His hands slide over my body, exploring, stroking softly in contrast to the sweet stabs of pleasure between my legs, the combination raising my need for him higher and higher.

"Cole," I murmur.

The air around us sizzles. "Can't hear you." He pulls out and slams back in again, greedily plunging, frantic with need.

"Yes," I cry out. I love seeing him this aroused, this needy. My hands race over his hot skin, sharing in his urgency, the intimacy between us.

Cole gives a low groan and crushes his hands through my hair. "I'm so close," he growls. The need in his voice sends me soaring, and my entire body squeezes. "Fuck, Reese."

I climax around his cock, my orgasm stronger than anything I've ever felt before. But I can't think about that right now as my sex throbs and pulses and I feel like I'm free-falling without a net. I whimper and hold on to Cole like my life depends on it.

"Breathe, Reese," he says and stills inside me, the intimacy in his tone sending a riot of emotions racing through me as I clench so hard I practically lose my vision. As he gives me a moment to recover, he moves my hair from my face. My lids flash open and when I catch the tender way he's looking at me my heart goes into my throat. "You good?" he asks.

I nod, too afraid to speak, too afraid of what I might say. I move against him, undulating my hips to let him know I'm ready for him again—want everything he has to give me. As my body quakes, I mentally kick myself for going off the pill. I want to feel him release inside me. The first thing I'm going to do when we return home is to go back on birth control. Wait!

Shit. I'm not thinking clearly. This ends when this trip is over and we go our separate ways.

He jerks his hips forward and our moans mingle, all thoughts of the pill forgotten. I lift to take him in deeper, and love the way his lids grow heavier like he's lost to everything except what the two of us are doing.

A new kind of need churns inside me, fueling my desires, pushing me close to the precipice once again.

I wrap my legs around his back and hug him with my thighs. His head goes back and his eyes close as he stills inside me. I take in his features, the strength of his body, the closeness between us.

"Come for me again, Reese," he commands, and just like that I let go, my body obeying his demands with another hot rush of heat between my legs. Honest to God, I never expected to come a third time, but the look on his face, and the command in his voice, pushed me over the edge again.

"Oh, fuck, Reese," he says. "I feel you."

"I feel you, too," I say, but never have I felt anything like this. I slide my hands around his back and tug until his mouth is on mine. We kiss, our tongues languidly sliding as we ride out our releases. On his last pulse, Cole collapses on top of me, his mouth going to my neck. His breath is so hot it's scalding my skin. I hold him to me. Holy hell. I feel a level of satisfaction I've never known. It's insane how good it is between us. I had no idea it could ever be this good.

Yes, you did.

Okay, maybe I did. Maybe I wanted this, thought about it once, twice or a million times over the years. But I sure as hell wasn't going to act on it. This is Cole. My best friend in the whole world. We hold each other for a long time, both lost in our own thoughts. His hand is on my arm, stroking softly, touching me in such a familiar way.

"Reese," he finally says, breaking the quiet as he pulls out of me.

His harsh breath flutters the hair on my neck, and I ache at the sudden loss of him inside me. "Yeah?"

"We good?" he asks, his voice rumbling against my ear.

"Yes," I say, pretty sure things will never be the same again.

"Still hate me?"

"More than ever."

"Hate you, too."

Chapter Four

COLE

I pace inside my hotel room, my mind racing a million miles an hour. I still can't believe I had sex with Reese. In a haunted cave. At the top of a mountain. Where anyone could have walked in on us.

It was fucking awesome.

I probably shouldn't have acted on my urges. I fought hard and long not to, tried to bank my desires, but fuck, I couldn't ignore the heat arcing between us for one more second. I tried. I really fucking did. The last thing I ever wanted to do was jeopardize our friendship. But holy hell, when she leaned into me, and I felt the need in her body reaching out to me, demanding attention, it snapped the last vestige of my control.

Yeah, I played with her, made it into a game and told her we could have epic sex, fulfill her vacation requirements, among other things, and go back to normal when the weekend was done.

No way in hell can we go back. Now that I've had a taste of

her, I want more. In fact, I want it all. Except that douchebag Jared did a total number on her, and she's off relationships. Not to mention I live two thousand miles away and I'm not the guy for her, can't give her what she wants in life. Fuck, my family's track record sucks, and I don't want to promise things I obviously can't give, which means I need to get my shit together right fucking now.

I walk to the window, pull back the curtain, and look at the dark beach below, lit only by the moon and stars. The waves lapping against the sandy shore call out to me. Maybe a good hard swim will help clear my thoughts so I can figure out how I can give her the fun she's seeking while on vacation and still walk away from this unscathed.

I drop the curtain, wipe the moisture from my brow, and fiddle with the air conditioner. No wonder it's so hot in the room—the damn thing isn't working. I reach for my phone to text Reese, when it pings in my hand. I read her text.

It's a million degrees in my room.

I respond with, *Air conditioner is broke.*

I can't freaking breathe.

Is little Reesey Piecey melting?

I'm dying.

Okay, let's get out of here, I suggest.

Swim?

I read the words, and from the corner of my eye, I see the ice bucket. A wicked, delicious idea forms. My thumbs fly over the screen. I know I should fucking put a stop to this. But how can I? This is Reese, and I want to make this vacation epic for her. She deserves that after douchebag Jared.

Good idea. Come on over.

I'll change and be right there.

I drop the phone, grab the bucket, and leave my door open for Reese. Following the sign for ice, I go to the second floor and fill the bucket. When I return to the room, I find Reese looking for me. I take a moment to just admire her from afar.

Hunger consumes me, and my cock registers every delicious detail of the gorgeous woman before me.

"Where the heck are you?" she's asking.

"Hey," I whisper and she turns.

"You scared me," she says, giving a breathy, intimate laugh as her hand goes to her chest. "Where were you?" she asks, no awkwardness between us after this afternoon. For a bit there, I was seriously worried there would be. But there's just warm familiarity, thanks to the incredible bond between us.

I lift the bucket. "Ice."

"What for?" Her eyes narrow in confusion as she plants her hands on her hips. The movement lifts her cover-up and exposes her creamy thighs. "I thought we were going for a swim."

I shut the door, set the lock, and without missing a beat I begin. "See, the thing is, the ocean water is too warm to do the job." I drop the bucket on the dresser, step up to her, and press my hand to her forehead. "In situations like this, we must get the body cooled down fast. Otherwise it could be lethal." I tap her arms. "Lift."

Without hesitation, her hands go in the air, and I stifle my chuckle at how eager she is to play along, even though she has no idea what kind of game it is. The trust Reese has in me is a pretty big fucking deal, and I'd never do anything to break it.

I grip the hem of her knit cover-up and pull it over her head. I exhale hard as I expose her body. I've seen her in a bathing suit a million times—heck I saw her naked just a few hours ago—but I could spend the rest of my life just staring at her, she's so beautiful.

I slide my hands down her arms, and little goose bumps form. "Your skin is very hot," I say. "As an adventure guide, I watch for signs of heat stroke in our clients."

"Oh." Lust moves into her eyes as they race over me, and her cheeks turn a soft shade of pink. My favorite color. "So, you're trained for this kind of thing?"

I step closer, tension bunching my muscles as I breathe in her scent. "Yeah."

"Tell me, how does an adventure guide cool people down when they find themselves in these dangerous kinds of situations?"

"Well," I say, and slide my hand around her back to untie her bathing suit. It flutters to the floor, and her chest rises and falls as her breathing changes. "First thing I need to do is get them naked."

She arches a dubious brow. "No clothes at all?"

"That's right."

She toys with the band on her bikini. "Not even a little bathing suit?"

"No clothes at all, Reese," I say very seriously.

"Okay." She straightens at the sternness in my voice. "You're the guide, so I trust you know what you're doing."

I grip her bikini bottoms and sink to my knees as I drag them to her ankles. I tap her legs, and she kicks off her flip-flops and lets me remove the slip of material. "That's better," I say, my mouth inches from her pretty pussy. I blow slightly, and her clit swells.

"But I...I don't feel better," she says, her voice a bit broken as I slide back up, trailing my hands over her curves.

"We're just getting started." I grip her shoulders and turn her, and when I see her gorgeous back and her soft round ass, I nearly pant like a damn dog.

"I think I'm actually getting hotter." She bends forward slightly to press her ass against me.

Yeah, me, too.

"I know just how to break this kind of fever." I put my mouth near her ear, and run my hands down her back until I'm cupping her sweet cheeks. I knead them for a second and then give her a little slap. She yelps, and I say, "Don't move."

She quivers, and it fuels my hunger as I step away to grab the bucket. I place it on the nightstand beside us, then fish out a cube and pop it into my mouth. I'm so goddamn hot and worked up, it begins to melt quickly.

I move back behind her and push her hair aside to expose the long column of her neck. "The best place to start the cooling process is right here," I say, and clamp the cube between my teeth. I run it along her neck and a little "ooh" comes out of her mouth on a breathless whisper.

The ice melts on her scalding body, and I trail my cold tongue over her trembling flesh and grab two more cubes.

"Where is the next best place?" she asks with a new urgency in her voice that strokes my dick and makes it impossibly harder.

"Let me show you."

I slide my hands around her and run the ice over her nipples. "Oh, my," she whispers. "That's so cold."

A rush of sexual energy hits so hard, my pulse kicks up a notch. "That's the idea." I slowly walk around her, and when I'm facing her, I circle her hard nipples. As the ice melts, water drips onto my bare feet. I keep rubbing until the cubes are nothing but small chips, then I toss them into my mouth and crunch on them. Reese wets her bottom lip, her eyes so full of playful lust that all I want to do is bury myself in her for the rest of the night.

The rest of my life.

She moves restlessly, going from one foot to the other as sexual tension crackles in the air. "I'm still not sure it's helping, though."

"Then I'm going to have to take drastic measures."

"Drastic?" Eyes wide, she goes still, totally into this game. "Will that be dangerous?"

I dip my head, my mouth close to hers. "Do you trust me?"

"You know I do."

I give her a little nudge and set her into motion. She walks backward toward the bed, and when the backs of her legs hit, I push on her shoulder. She falls onto the mattress, and I stare down at her. The sight is picture perfect, and I can't wait to put my mouth on her again.

She writhes and I crack the window to let the ocean breeze circulate through the warm room.

"Widen your legs," I command. "I need to assess you before we go any farther."

She does as I ask, and my gaze goes to her pretty pink pussy, the dampness glistening in the lamplight. With my mouth salivating, I step up to her, run my hand up her thigh, and push a thick finger into her sweetness.

"Oh, my," she says. "Is this how you assess everyone?"

"Not usually. But with the kind of heat you seem to be experiencing, I want to be thorough and check your temperature—external and internal—to see exactly what I'm dealing with."

"And?"

"It's not good, Reese."

"Oh, no."

I scrub my face and shake my head. "It's worse than I thought."

"What can we do?"

"I'm going to ice you down. Everywhere."

"What if that doesn't work?" She blinks as she really gets into this. "I'm scared, Cole."

"Don't be scared. You know I'm going to take really good care of you." I grab a cube, climb onto the bed, and slide between her legs. "Open really wide for me now." She stretches her legs open and her sweet pussy lips spread. Fuck, that's so pretty. I nod toward the headboard. "Hold on to those slats tight, and no matter what, don't let go."

Beginning at her ankle, I run the ice up her leg, and she quivers beneath me. I come close to her sex but never touch. Instead I go to the other leg, and she grumbles as I tease her. When the cube melts, I grab another and toss it into my mouth. I follow the wet path on her leg, but this time, bury my face between her thighs. Her hips lift when I center the cube on her scalding-hot clit, and it practically sizzles as I bathe it in ice.

"Oh, yes," she cries out, moving against my mouth. "I think it's helping," she adds, impatience in her voice. Christ, I love how she reacts to me, how desperate she is for so much more.

I stick my hand in the bucket to cool my fingers, then slide one inside her. "Cole," she murmurs, and I must admit, hearing my name roll off her lips when my fingers are inside her is a total fucking turn-on. "That feels so good."

I lick and nibble and fuck her with my finger until she's gyrating beneath me. When the ice melts, I reach for more and drag it over her sex, probing her opening. Her entire body is quaking, and my dick is so hard I'm about to explode. I push another finger inside and she tightens around me as I swirl through her slick heat. Fuck, that's so good. I bring her higher and higher but never take her over. No, I want to be inside her when she comes. I want to feel her squeeze my cock, and have her hot juices drip over my balls.

I take in the perspiration beading on her forehead. "You're burning up. I'm going to let off some more steam before you reach the boiling point."

"How?" she pants.

"I have no choice but to put my cock in you."

She nods quickly, her eyes alive with anticipation. "If you think that will work."

"I'm certain of it." I pull my fingers from her sex and remove my clothes quickly, then snatch a condom from my nightstand and reposition myself between her legs.

She whimpers. "I want you to do whatever is necessary to cool me down, Cole."

I roll the condom on and watch her breasts move as she writhes. Damn, I want my mouth on them. I look at her hands, her knuckles white as she holds the headboard slats.

"Let go." She does as I ask and I tug on her hand until she's seated. I slide in behind her, and press my back to the headboard. "Come here." She turns and straddles me, and I draw one hard bud into my mouth as I guide her onto my stiff cock. As her muscles close around me, I bite down on her nipple, and she convulses.

I grip her rib cage, sweep my thumbs over her breasts, and her hands go to my hair. She runs her fingers through it as I lift her, up and down, up and down, until my heart is hammering so hard I think it might break a fucking rib.

I slam into her, and when she moans, I close my eyes and lose myself in her sweetness. Her heat spreads through my body and takes me right there, so fucking fast, but I don't want to come just yet. I continue to power into her, and her breasts jiggle against my chest as I draw her mouth to mine for a hungry kiss.

Her hands go to my shoulders, sweep across my skin, and my blood rushes faster. I love the way she touches me. Fuck, I never want to be touched by anyone but her ever again.

"Cole," she says, her body trembling from head to toe. "I'm...I'm..."

Her hot release drips down my cock. My balls pull up into my body and I know I'm a goner. "Reese," I murmur and cup the back of her head as I press my mouth against her neck. "That's it. Come all over my cock. Let me feel you."

She trembles and breaks around me and I hold her and absorb her tremors as she lets go. Before she completely finishes, I roll my hips so my pelvis brushes against her clit. She gives a little gasp and clenches even harder as I prolong her pleasure.

"Yesss," she hisses, and I grab her hips and hold her down on me as she shudders in surrender. Her deeply satisfied eyes meet mine and my heart misses a beat. I put that look on her face. Me. My chest swells with smug satisfaction.

"I love making you come," I say and brush her hair from her shoulders as sweat breaks out on my body. "I love seeing the look on your face as you let go for me." As soon as the words leave my mouth, pressure builds between my legs and comes to a peak. Her muscles tighten around my cock and I settle my mouth on her.

"Fuck, Reese," I say between hot, hungry kisses. I pull her against my body and climax high inside her. Air rips from my lungs as my cock pulses and throbs with the hot flow of release. I let loose a low growl of sexual satisfaction, and it mingles with the soft erotic sounds rising in her throat. Christ almighty, sex with her gets better every single time.

"Cole," she murmurs as I pulse inside her hot pussy, and her trembling hands tug at me like she can't get me close enough. I pant and try to catch my breath as our bodies mold together as one. I hold her so tight, crush her to me so hard,

I'm sure she can't breathe, but I can't let go.

Won't let go.

A sound catches in her throat, and I reluctantly loosen my hold so I can see her. Her eyes are shut and her mouth is pressed tight. My heart jumps into my throat as panic zings through me. I want to give her what she wants, but I pray to fucking God it doesn't fuck over everything between us.

Chapter Five

Sunlight pours in through the open curtains, and I lay there completely naked in Cole's bed, enjoying the early morning sea breeze through the cracked window. My God, what would the girls think if they ever found out I was having sex with my best friend. I know a few of them have hit on Cole over the years, have tried to get him exactly where I have him right now, but he always turned them down. I was never sure why, but I'm kind of glad that he did.

I shift to my side and look at the sleeping man beside me. My breath catches as lust punches into my stomach. Honest to God, he's so handsome, yet so boyish-looking in his sleep that it's all I can do not to touch him, to snuggle in close and hope for a repeat of last night. It's not the first time we've slept in the same bed. Heck, when we were younger, he used to sneak in through my bedroom window whenever it stormed just to hold me. But last night is definitely the first time we had sex in one.

Not wanting to wake him, I shift on the mattress carefully, and muscles I haven't used in a long time ache. But it's a good ache, a great reminder of all the naughty things I've been doing with Cole. I can't believe how thorough he is in bed, what an amazing lover he is. It's like he is so attuned with my body he knows just how I like to be touched, what I need to push me over the edge. I could so get used to being with Cole like this.

As I think about that, my bliss disappears. No way does Cole want to move past a sexual relationship. He told me, when we return home, things go back to normal. He has total commitment issues. Heck, he doesn't have sex with the same person more than once. Then again, we've had sex a few times already. But he's just allowing me to play out a fantasy, fulfill the requirements of my dossier. Epic sex. That's all this is. My best friend, who's always been there for me, is just once again stepping in to help me out.

I tiptoe to the bathroom and turn on the shower. Even though I don't want to wash his warm scent from my body, after our passionate night of sex, I need to get cleaned up and ready for today's adventure. Spending a lazy day in bed with him sounds much better than a five-hour drive to go on a wildlife tour, however. But my sponsor paid a lot for this vacation, and it wouldn't be fair to let it go to waste.

I open the sliding glass door and climb into the large tiled area. The hot spray feels glorious against my chafed skin, compliments of the scruff on Cole's chin. I tilt my head back and close my eyes. I stand like that for a long time and try not to think about what it will be like for Cole and me when we leave here. I hear a noise and my lids flutter open to find the shower door cracked and a naked Cole watching me. I gasp as our gazes collide.

"How long have you been standing there," I ask, my breath a little harder to capture as I take in his ripped body.

"Long enough." Eyes ablaze with heat and hunger, he looks down, and I follow his gaze to his cock.

I take in the long, hard length of him, and my body responds with a quiver. "Oh," is all I can manage to get out as the air around us charges with sexual energy.

"Yeah, oh." He grins. "Can *we* join you?"

"You think there's enough room for the two of you in here," I tease.

"I think so."

"If not, we'll have to a find a way to deflate little Cole."

He laughs. "Little Cole?"

If I knew what was good for me, I'd put an end to this weekend right now, get out while the getting was good. But I don't have the strength to deny myself what I really want, even though it goes against my best interest, so I crook my finger, and Cole climbs in. He slides big hands around my body, and I sag against him, his chest to my back, where I feel his strong heartbeat pound into my shoulder blade. I move against him, unable to get close enough as my breasts grow hot and achy. Why does it always feel so good to be in his arms? Why did I feel so lost when he left New York?

He puts his mouth to my ear, his hands caressing my bare skin. "How do you feel?"

"Good," I say, even though my emotions are a chaotic mess.

"Just good?" His voice is playful as he grips my rib cage, his index fingers brushing my breasts. They swell beneath the rough pads of his thumbs and I moan, my body aching for something far more intimate. "Better?"

Playing along, I say. "Maybe just a bit."

"Oh, is that right." He splays his fingers and slides his hand down over my stomach. He cups my mound and squeezes, and I lean forward slightly to rub my ass against his cock, a vicious little tease.

"How do *you* feel?" I ask in return.

"You tell me." He grips his cock, and from behind slides it between my thighs.

"Hard," I say, and he laughs.

"Yeah." He widens my sex lips and runs his finger over me, circling my clit, but never touching. My temperature rises, and my pulse kicks up a notch. "Still just 'good'?"

"Still just good," I lie, and undulate my hips to massage his erection and try to force his fingers inside me.

"Let's see what I can do about that." He lightly strokes my clit and I whimper.

"Yesss," I hiss.

He takes his hands away, his breath hot on my ear. "That sounds like it's better than just good."

"Cole," I say and move against him. "More."

"More of this?" he asks and strokes my clit.

"Yes, more of this," I say and shake with sexual need.

"It's good, huh?"

"Really good."

His hand slides lower and he inserts a finger. I practically come the instant he touches me. He pushes inside, strokes me deep, and rubs my clit with the top of his palm. His mouth goes to my neck, and he presses his hot lips to my wet skin. Sparks shoot through me, and I want to move, turn around and take his cock into my hands, but he seems to have other ideas.

Commanding yet soft, he grips the back of my neck and urges me forward, bending me at the waist as he walks me to the tiled wall opposite the hot spray. "Hands right here," he growls, his voice deeper, rougher. He captures my wrists and flattens my palms on the wall, then nudges my feet with his to adjust my stance. "Don't move," he says, his breath playing down my spine. My entire body quivers as I offer myself up to him this way. He rubs my ass then gives it a little slap.

As a tremble moves through me, I hear the door sliding open and look at him over my shoulder. I whimper as he disappears from the stall. What the hell is he doing? I wait for a second as he hovers near the bathroom counter, and when I see him coming back, sliding a rubber over his hard cock, a surge of excitement races through me.

He steps back up to me, and he grips my hips. "Let's see if I can make you feel *really* good," he says, the heat in his voice exciting me even more. He positions his cock between my legs, rubs it over my clit until I'm near delirious, then probes my entrance. In one quick thrust, he drives into me. Oh, yes! I brace my hands on the wall as my legs go weak.

"I got you," he murmurs, his arm circling my waist to hold me.

He inches out of me, then slides in, seating himself inside. "Feels so good," I cry out.

"How does this feel?" His hips power forward, penetrating me deeper than ever before.

I claw at the wall. "Yes," I groan. "More."

He pulls out only to slam back in again. I can feel the tension rising in him as he pounds into me, reaching a fevered pitch that sends me soaring. My entire body quivers uncontrollably.

I'm a hot, trembling mess as my muscles spasm and suck him in deeper. Sex with your best friend might be wrong, but holy hell, it feels so right. Dizzy, wild, feverish with need, I rear back and meet each thrust. He reaches between my legs and applies pressure to my clit, teasing and tormenting an orgasm right out of me. Pressure builds, reaches dangerous proportions, and I moan and buck, wanting more…wanting everything.

"That's it," Cole says as an explosion tears through me.

"Cole," I cry out, my entire body vibrating around his hard cock.

"You feel so good," he murmurs, his voice falling over me. He grips my hips and holds tight as he releases high inside me. His pleasure resonates through me and brings on another hot flow of release. After depleting himself, he leans over me and dusts light kisses over my shoulder as I ride out the waves.

I gasp, but can't seem to fill my lungs. "Breathe, Reese," he says as he pulls out of me and puts his hands on my shoulders to spin me around. He pushes my hair from my shoulders and breathes with me. His gaze never leaves mine as he holds me until I'm no longer gasping. My heart pinches at the way he's always taking care of me, making me feel special, important to him.

He dispenses with the condom, then reaches for me. "Come here."

He turns us and walks backward until I'm under the hot spray. He grabs the soap, runs it over my body, then uses it on himself. All I can seem to do is stand there, lost in the haze of euphoric sex, and watch him.

After rinsing us both down, he turns off the spray, and I hear a knock on the door. I tense. Cripes, could it be the neighbors complaining at the noise level in room 201?

"Who could that be?" I ask quietly

"Room service."

What a nice surprise. "When did you order that?"

"Before joining you in here." He opens the steamy sliding door, reaches behind him to capture one of my hands, and guides me out. I wring out my wet hair quickly and follow him. Cole grabs a big fluffy towel and throws it around my shoulders. His thumb goes to my chin, and he lifts my head until my lips are poised open.

He dips his head and gives me a kiss so full of emotion and tenderness that I grow needy for him again. My heart clenches, everything I feel for this man right there on the surface, threatening to bring tears. Honest to God, I've never experienced such a deep level of intimacy with anyone before. Is it because this is Cole, my best friend, or is there more going on between us?

I slide my arms around his waist and hold him so I don't sink to the floor in a heap of quivering need. Looking for a distraction—something, anything to get my mind off the riot of emotions coursing through me—I glance at the torn foil on the counter.

"How lucky that you just happened to find a condom on the counter," I say.

He inches back. "Yeah, I know, right?"

"If you ask me, I think you put it there on purpose. That you had every intention of climbing in here and having your way with me."

His grin is crooked and adorable. "Then I won't ask," he says. He reaches around me to give my ass a fast slap. "Stay in here. I'll get the door and let you know when the coast is clear."

"I can come with you."

He knots a towel around his waist. "No, don't. You're only in a towel."

"I don't care."

"I do."

At first I think he's kidding, then I notice there is no amusement in his voice. "It covers more than my bathing suit, Cole."

His jaw clenches. "Yeah, and you look as sexy as hell in both, and I don't want the delivery guy gawking at you, okay?"

I look as sexy as hell in both?

I let loose an exaggerated breath and fight valiantly to suppress the things I'm feeling for this man. "Okay, fine," I say, deciding to stay in the bathroom to chew on that as Cole goes to let in room service.

I wait behind the door, and when I hear Cole give the guy

a tip and shut and lock the main door, I step into the room. When I see the kitchen has delivered all my favorite breakfast foods, my heart goes a little wobbly. Would Jared have even known all my favorites? Was it possible that I *had* been trying to change him into someone like…oh, shit.

I am in so much trouble here. Cole is the man I was trying to turn Jared into. The man I've always wanted to be with. But he's not a guy to commit, and his life is in Colorado. If I ask him to stay—and there's no saying he'd want that, anyway—I'd be trying to change him, too, and that would lead to resentment and heartache.

Maybe I need to put a stop to this affair right now.

"Cole—"

"Come on, I'm starved," Cole says, and drops his towel like getting naked in front of me is now the most natural thing in the world. I stare as he tugs on a pair of jeans and zips them up.

With my thoughts running a million miles an hour, I let my towel fall to the floor. I glance around for something to wear, but since I came to his room last night dressed only in a bathing suit and white knit cover-up, it's all I have to wear this morning. I grab the see-through dress and slip into it. It does little to hide my body, and I adjust it when one of my nipples pokes through.

Cole sets the plates out on the small table. I sit in one of the chairs, and Cole fixes my coffee with cream and one sugar. I take a much-needed sip.

"Mm, heaven," I whisper, wanting to talk to him but not knowing how to start or what to say. The truth is part of me knows I need to stop this madness, but there is another part of me that wants to finish out this weekend with him.

He dishes up the hotcakes, bacon, fruit, and maple syrup. "Eat. You're going to need your energy for a long day."

I reach for my fork. "If I eat all this, I'm going to need a nap."

"You can nap on the bus."

I groan. "I'm not looking forward to a five-hour bus ride."

"I know, but it will be worth it. This adventure is right up your alley."

"I guess I am kind of looking forward to seeing the endangered species in their home. I'm glad they're being taken care of properly."

Cole takes a sip of black coffee, his face going serious as he chews on a piece of bacon. "Remember when we were kids, and you always talked about opening your own shelter for rescue dogs?"

"Yeah."

"You don't talk about that anymore."

I shrug. "Work is busy, and there just aren't enough hours in the day for me to find a place or get things in order."

"So, you'd still like to do that."

I nod. "Yeah, I would."

"What was it you wanted to call it? Bed and Barkfest?"

I laugh. "I can't believe you remember that."

His bare foot touches mine beneath the table. "I remember everything, Reese."

So, do I.

"Tell me about your job in Colorado," I say, remembering the times he talked about opening his own adventure camp. Is that something he still thinks about?

His face lights with a smile, and it's clear he loves what he does. No surprise there. Unlike me, Cole always was an adrenaline junkie who needed adventure to thrive.

"I love it." He gives a slow shake of his head. "The rapids, the scenery, the steep stretches, and the whitewater." He opens his hands wide. "It's unlike anything you've ever seen. For most people, it's a once-in-a-lifetime adventure, and I get to do it every week. How lucky am I, right?"

"Very," I say, unease moving through me. I keep telling myself I'm a big girl and don't need Cole, but it's going to kill me when he leaves again.

"One of the trips includes camping and visiting a cattle ranch. You should come visit. I'll take you out."

"No, thanks," I say quickly.

"One of the rafting trips includes horseback riding. You'd love that."

"Can I skip the rafting and just do the horseback riding?"

He pops a piece of bacon into his mouth and grins. "Yeah, you can do that, Reesey Piecey. But come on, you went shark diving. It's all anticlimactic after that."

As if on cue, my nipple pops out again, and Cole clears his throat. "Speaking of climactic," he says, and I readjust myself to hide my turgid nipple.

As much as I like where his mind is going, I point at his breakfast. "Hurry up and eat. We have a bus to catch in thirty minutes."

"I'll be fast," he says.

"Cole," I warn.

He laughs and takes a swig of coffee. "Hey, can't blame a guy for trying."

No, I can't. He's a guy and guys think about sex. All. The. Time. Even if this was more than that for him, which it's not, our lives are in two different places. Mine, New York. His, Colorado. I would never ask him to give that up, or try to change him.

Chapter Six

COLE

After a long bus ride through the awesome scenery of the plains and cliffs of desert-like Klein Karoo, we arrive at our destination in the Western Cape. As we all climb off and stretch out our legs, we're greeted by our guide and led to our hotel room to get ourselves settled before the tour of the endangered species ranch.

My room is next to Reese's. I can't help but think it's a waste of money. We could have spared whoever sponsored this trip the cost of two rooms and just shared one. We've done that numerous times, even when we weren't sleeping together.

I splash some water on my face and change into a clean shirt and shorts. Twenty minutes later, I knock on Reese's door, and when it swings open, it takes every ounce of strength I have not to push inside, lock the door behind us, and spend the next two days in her bed.

"Are you ready?" she asks, her eyes wide with excitement.

I back up and wave for her to move past me. As much as I like my idea of staying in, she's been talking nonstop about visiting the Cango Wildlife Ranch and seeing all the endangered species. Will she be brave enough to get her picture taken with a cheetah, or will she climb into my arms again, frightened half to death? As I mull that over, I do wonder why the friend who drew her name is putting her in situations that might frighten her. We all know she doesn't like to step out of her comfort zone. Could that be why they wanted me here with her? Or was there another reason entirely. Hell, maybe they thought we were meant to be together, and this was their way of trying to make it happen. Nah, couldn't be that. Right?

Reese closes her door and breezes past me into the hall, and I catch the fresh scent of her shampoo. Makeup free, dressed in shorts and a T-shirt with her hair pulled back into a ponytail, she's the quintessential girl-next-door, and I've never seen her look more stunning.

We take the two flights of stairs to the main level and find a few others milling about, waiting for the jeep to pick us up and take us the short distance to the ranch. I flip through a brochure, then glance around and take in the eclectic mix of people as Reese speaks to a middle-aged woman about the trip. They're discussing the animal encounters and which species they'd like to meet up close and personal.

Grinning, I glance outside, but when I see some douchebag looking at Reese, I feel a possessive tug in my gut. I take a deep breath and let it out slowly. I'd like nothing more than to punch the guy in the face, but Christ, what right do I have to take down every guy who looks at her the wrong way. Or the right way. Or any fucking way at all.

Just then, a horn sounds, and we all make our way outside. Reese and I climb into the back of an open-air jeep that has been modified to seat nine people. During the short jaunt to the ranch, the driver gives us an educational briefing, discussing the conservation and breeding programs, and how they use interaction with certain ambassador animals to raise awareness, and that guests who have an encounter are more likely to react positively toward conservation issues. As the driver continues to talk, I pull out my phone and take a picture of Reese.

She blinks and whacks me. "What did you do that for?"

"Wanted to capture the moment."

"Save your space, and take pictures of the scenery and animals, not me."

I think about the shark diving video we've yet to see and turn my attention to the brochure. I hold it up and point to the crocodile cage diving. "Want to do that?" She gives a slow shake of her head.

"I think I've done enough cage diving for a lifetime," she says.

I laugh, and the jeep comes to a stop at the ranch. I hop from the backseat, put my arms around Reese's waist, and help her out. The staff tells us we'll have a guided tour and then two hours to explore on our own. Within seconds, the tour guide Angela, dressed in a brown uniform with *Cango* emblazed on the T-shirt, arrives and leads us through a huge set of alligator teeth, aka the door to the park.

Reese pauses before the entrance. "If this is a sign of things to come…" she whispers.

"Don't worry—"

"I know," she says. "You won't let anything happen to me."

"Right. Come on." I capture her hand and give a little tug to set her into motion. We follow the guide, and she leads us through the Valley of Ancients to view a variety of animals and reptiles. Then we cross a catwalk over a large natural enclosure, home to cheetahs, lions, leopards, and rare snow-white tigers.

Every time I glance at Reese, I grin and snap a few more pictures without her knowledge. I should be documenting the animals for her so she can enjoy them later, but I can't keep my eyes off her. She is so totally in her element, and I love being here to capture the moment.

Little Reesey Piecey has wanted to be a vet since we were kids, and she talked forever about opening her very own rescue shelter. That's probably why this conservation is so fascinating to her. Shit, maybe her dream could have come true if I'd stayed home to help her instead of fucking off to Colorado.

"Now what everyone is waiting for," Angela says, folding her hands in front of her chest. "Up close and personal interaction with the animals." Angela turns and says, "Follow me."

Reese makes a nervous sound, and I'm about to pull her to me when the mouth-breather who'd been watching her earlier steps up to her.

"Nothing to worry about," he says and cracks his knuckles.

"No?" she asks. "You've done it."

"Not here, but I've totally done it before. Practically pet a cheetah in the wild."

Yeah, right, buddy.

"That's not safe," Reese says, clearly not impressed, and I try not to laugh. "You should never interfere with an animal in its natural habitat. Here, well, it's different."

"I have a way with wild things," he says, his gaze dropping to Reese's mouth. "I know just how to tame them. Come on. Stick with me. I'll show you."

Like fuck.

Reese opens her mouth, and from the fire in her eyes, I know she's offended. Even though she can take care of herself, I really like that role. Yeah, I might be a possessive ass, but this is Reese, and I can't help it.

"You ready, babe," I ask and slide my arm around her waist.

The guy puffs out his steroid-enhanced chest and glares at me. "She's afraid, so she's coming with me so I can protect her."

I seriously know I'm acting like a jerk. If I don't cool it, I'm going to scare her off. I need to take things slow, let her get used to the idea of being mine long term before I go acting all fucking caveman with her.

Long term?

Where the hell had that thought come from?

I'm not sure, but now that it's out there, fuck yeah, I want a long term with her.

"Oh, I'm pretty sure she's not. If my fiancée needs anything, I'll be the one to give it to her."

Reese, my fiancée?

Damned if I don't like the sound of that. Yeah, I might come from a long line of bastards that could never commit, who always ended up hurting the women in my family, but fuck family heritage. I'm a better man than that, and this is Reese—I'd never, ever do anything to hurt her. She comes first and foremost, always has, and that's never going to change.

Two sets of eyes zero in on me. I steal a quick glance at Reese, giving her a minute to think on that, to get used to the idea. Mouth-breather narrows his brow, doing his best imitation of the missing link as he tries to sort that one through. His gaze goes from Reese's empty finger to me.

"Your fiancée?"

"That's right," I say, and hold Reese tighter. She sags into me and puts her hand on my chest.

The guy stares at me for a minute. I'm pretty sure he's debating whether to call me out on my lie. Maybe even punching me in the face from a steroid-induced rage. What-the-fuck-ever. He might be a big bastard, but I can hold my own.

"Not worth it," the guy says, and stomps off to follow the crowd.

Reese angles her head, and when I glance at her, she doesn't seem too pleased with me.

"What did you do that for?"

"That guy was all wrong for you," I say as she pushes away from me.

"No kidding." She shakes her head and looks at the sky. I follow her gaze to see the sun disappear behind a bank of dark clouds. Shit. I hope to God we don't have a storm. They always bring back painful memories for Reese, and I want her to have only great memories from this trip. "Why am I such a jerk magnet, Cole?" She rubs her forehead. "Do I have a sign on me or something?"

I frown and give her hand a reassuring squeeze. "I'm sorry Jared hurt you. But not all guys are douchebags."

She laughs and jerks her thumb toward the guy stomping away, the ground practically rumbling beneath his feet. "You're going to tell me that after Mr. Steroid pretty much told me I was a wild thing he wanted to tame?"

I rub my knuckles along her arm. "Reese," I say, and pitch my voice low. "There are good guys out there."

She snorts and turns toward the group walking toward the cheetah pen. "When you find one, let me know."

I push my hair from my forehead, and it takes all I have not to blurt out how I feel. But I'm too fucking worried I might ruin things between us. "I'm not a bad guy, you know."

She stops and looks at me, a deep sadness on her face. "I know, Cole. I'm sorry. I didn't mean to say you were." She goes quiet and looks down at her feet. I step up to her, touch her chin, and angle it until she's looking at me.

"What?" I ask.

"Why did you come on this trip with me?"

"You needed me."

She nods and gives me a smile, but I can tell it's forced. Then she lightly punches me on the arm. "I can take care of myself, whether you and the girls think so or not."

"What are you talking about?"

She gives a deep sigh. "I get it. Whoever sponsored this trip thought I couldn't do it without you. I can, Cole. I'm quite capable of taking care of myself. I don't need you here." She folds her arms the way she always does when she's serious about something. "I don't think we should sleep with each other anymore."

Fuck no. What is going on?

I reach for her, but she steps back. "Reese—"

"Also, when this trip is over, you need to go back to Colorado. You don't need to stay in New York any longer."

I stand there staring at her, feeling like she just punched through my chest and tore out my heart. "Reese," I say and reach for her. "I just...I..."

She takes another step back, putting more distance between us, physically and emotionally. "I know. I know. You just want to take care of me. But you can stop."

Love you.

That's what I was going to say, that I fucking love her.

My fucking God, I love her. I always have.

"You want me to go?" I ask instead, a pounding beginning at the base of my neck and racing through my skull.

"Yes, and I really don't want to talk about this anymore." She pulls from me and walks away.

I fist my hair as she retreats. What the fuck is going on? One minute we're laughing and having fun, the next she's telling me to go back to Colorado because it's where I belong. She's so wrong, on so many fucking levels. Where I belong is in New York with her. Yeah, I might be an adrenaline junkie, but a life with Reese is the adventure I want. She makes me a better man, better than any of the men in my family, and I'd spend a lifetime treasuring her. Yet now she doesn't even want me in the same state as her anymore.

Not only am I going to lose the woman I love, but I'm also going to lose my very best friend, all because I couldn't keep my hands to myself.

Stupid. Fucking. Asshole.

Chapter Seven

Reese

With my stomach twisted into knots, I pace my room, hating how mean I was to Cole today. But God, I had to be. No way do I want him to give up his life because he thinks he has to take care of me, little old Reesey Piecey, who can't function without him. I'd never try to change him, never want him to come to resent me for it like Jared did. And obviously, I was trying to change Jared to be more like Cole because I love him. I've always loved him. The truth is I *can* function without him. I just don't want to.

I wipe away a runaway tear and place my hand on my stomach as nausea grips me. I love Cole so freaking much, and even though he might never talk to me again, and the loss of our friendship will shatter me completely, I had to push him away for his own good. He came back because I needed him, not because he wanted me.

You're just friends, Reese.

Friends who have really great sex, but friends nonetheless.

And it's time he went back to his life. When it comes right down to it, Cole hates working in construction with his uncle. He's built for adventure, like hiking the Colorado Mountains, white water rafting in the rivers…back-bending orgasms.

He was only having sex with me because my trip was supposed to be about finding a guy and sleeping with him. Yeah, sure, he seemed to enjoy it, too, but he's always there to protect me, help me out, and give me what I need. That's what the sex was all about, considering he only ever treated me as a buddy, one of the guys, before this trip.

I hear a distant rumble and walk to my window to peek out the curtains. Rain pelts the glass, and a quiver moves through me. God, I hate storms. Not just because they're loud and frightening, but also because when I was a kid, lightning struck my grandmother's house and she fell down the stairs during the blackout while trying to get to me. Finding her lifeless body that night still haunts me. Another roar of thunder backs me away from the window, and old, painful memories resurface.

Lightning brightens the sky, and I hurry to the bed and slide under the covers. I'm sitting there, counting the seconds between the light and thunder, when someone knocks on my door. I hug myself, hoping it's Cole as much as I hope it's not. I need to make a clean break from him, for both our sakes.

"Who is it?"

"It's me."

Cole.

"What's up?" I ask, trying for casual, like I'm perfectly fine.

A moment of silence and then, "Open the door, Reese."

Yeah, okay, so trying to pretend anything with Cole is a waste of time. He can always see right through me. It does make me wonder, though. Will he see through what I'm doing, the reason I'm pushing him away? What would he do if he knew how I really felt? Hop on the next bus and run for cover?

I sit there for a moment, toying with the blankets, but when the night sky lights up again, I jump from the bed and dash across the room. I pull the door open, and when I see the tender, caring way Cole is looking at me as he pulls me into his arms, my heart nearly breaks into a million tiny pieces. He guides me to my bed and doesn't bother to ask if I'm okay. He knows I'm not. He pulls the blankets down.

"Get in."

Dressed only in my thigh-high nightgown—*sans* panties—I slide in without a word, and Cole circles the bed. He tears off his jeans, and with only his boxer shorts on, crawls in next to me. He fixes the blankets around us and pulls me to him, spooning me from behind. His heat reaches out to me, his hands comforting as they hold me. My pulse crashes against my neck as I take comfort in his presence. It's hard to believe that after the way I treated him, he's here, holding me, soothing me, taking care of me. I don't deserve this after the way I pushed him away, physically and emotionally.

"Cole," I begin, though I have no idea what it is I want to say.

"It's okay, Reese," he says, and I wonder if he knows I'm trying to apologize for my behavior. "I've got you. You're safe."

He strokes my hair, pushing it from my shoulder, and I can feel his breath hot on my neck. Lightning strikes again, and even though I know I'm safe with him, I stiffen and shimmy closer, desperate for a deeper connection, even though I know better. But that's when I realize he's stiff, too—between the legs.

Oh, God, this is bad, so bad, but I can't help it. I want him again. I want to feel him inside me just one more time. I close my eyes and fight an internal war between right and wrong, but that doesn't stop my body from reacting to his.

Maybe I should go for it. If he's going back to Colorado, and I might never see him again, might have destroyed our friendship, maybe I should have this one last night with him. Farewell-sex between best friends.

"Cole."

"Yeah."

Run away, Reese.

"Remember when we were teens and you used to sneak into my room during storms."

"Uh huh."

Heartache be damned.

"You used to play games with me. Get me talking about things to distract me."

"Do you want to play a game, Reese?" he asks, his voice so deep it curls though me and ignites every nerve in my body.

"Yeah, I thought maybe we could do something to distract me."

He goes still. Too still, and my heart thunders. After today, he should push me away, tell me to go to hell. I inch away from him, expecting him to do just that, but when I turn to see him, and I catch the fire in his eyes, I take a quick breath. The man I know is funny and playful, and I'm sure I've never seen him look so intense before.

Maybe this is a bad idea.

I draw a shaky breath, and I'm about to say so when he pulls me underneath him. His lips come down on mine, and I moan as his tongue slides in. His kisses are slower and softer, a steady deepening that is different from before but every bit as profound. I tremble with the things I feel for him, the love that runs so deep.

He pulls back and touches my hair. "Did that work?" he asks.

"Yes," I whisper with effort.

His gaze moves over mine. "So, kissing works as a distraction?"

I try to speak but can only nod as my voice catches in my throat.

He runs his fingers along my neck, a soft tickle, and I quiver beneath his intimate touch. "If I kissed you here, do you think that would that work, too?"

"Yes," I croak. "I'm pretty sure."

His lips go to my neck, warm, soft, and so achingly tender I could die. He brushes his wet mouth over my flesh and shimmies lower. His hands slide gently down my body and grip the hem of my nightie. His hot breath warms me as he pulls up the slip of material. He doesn't need to ask me to sit up. I know instinctively what he wants, just like he always knows what I need. I lift, and he pulls the silk over my head, exposing me completely.

His gaze moves over my body, and he briefly pinches his eyes shut like he's in total freaking agony. My pulse speeds up.

"Cole?" I ask and reach for him. I know I'm being selfish, putting my current needs before Cole's, but I'm not about to continue with this if it's something he doesn't want to do.

"What about here, Reese?" he asks, running his thumb over my nipple. "If I kissed you here would it help?"

My brain shuts down as he caresses me. "Yes, please."

He grins at that and flattens his tongue over my tight nipple. The soft lick sends me flying to the moon, and I arch into him. I touch his shoulders, run my fingers over his hard muscles, and his body ripples under my touch.

I widen my legs, opening for him, welcoming him to my body. He takes a gulping breath and kisses a path to my sex, languidly running the soft blade of his tongue over my belly. He settles himself between my legs and pets my sex. I nearly purr.

"You think if I kiss you here it will help?"

"I think it will really help," I say.

He gives me a soft lick and widens my lips with the tip of his tongue. Heat flashes through me, making me dizzy. With a tongue that is hot and slick, he licks and sucks and pleasures me until I'm shaking all over. As my climax builds, I tighten under his caress, and he traces the length of my sex with his tongue before inserting a finger. Good God, he is such a generous lover, taking his time with me, but I ache to feel his hard flesh inside me. Honest to God, I have no idea how I'll ever be with another man after him.

His hard length presses against my leg, and I moan, desperate for more. His finger delves deeper, taking me higher, gifting me with a pleasure so intense it's almost painful.

I touch my breasts, and he slides one hand up my belly and closes his big palm over mine, and together we knead gently. I whimper and toss my head from side to side, as my clit throbs under his tongue.

"You want my cock in here?" he asks, moving his finger in and out of my slick core.

"Yes," I moan.

His fingers press deeper, harder, increasing the tension until I can no longer hold on. "Just like that," I cry out.

"Come for me, Reese. Show me how much you want my cock."

He pushes another finger in, and I shatter beneath his touch. As my pleasure spikes, the entire world closes in on me, and the flashes before my eyes have nothing to do with the storm raging outside.

He stays between my legs until I stop clenching, then his fingers and mouth abandon my sex, and he climbs up my body. I stroke his back and tremble with anticipation. I shift until his cock is right there. All I need is for him to piston forward and enter me.

"Shit," he says. "We can't do this." My heart crashes. Oh,

God, he doesn't want this. I take a quick second to berate myself. I never, ever should have initiated this, tonight or the first time in the cave. I'm about to scramble away when he says. "I'm out of condoms."

When I can breathe again, I say, "It's okay. I don't want to use one, anyway."

His gaze moves over my face, the tenderness in his eyes touching me more deeply than anything before. "Reese?"

I touch his cheek and he leans into my hand. "I want to feel you, Cole. I'm clean."

"I'm clean, too. I've never had sex without protection." He shakes his head and his hair falls into his eyes. "But you went off the pill. To give your body a break, remember?"

"How do you…" I begin and then stop and shake my head. This is Cole, and he seems to know everything about me. "I know where I am in my cycle and my chances of getting pregnant are low."

He cups the side of my head and drops a soft kiss onto my mouth. "If it's what you really want." Another soft kiss. And another.

"Only if you do."

He peppers more tender kisses over my face and whispers, "Yeah, I do."

He positions himself at my opening and closes his mouth over mine as he slowly rubs his cock over my sex. I arch into him.

"More," I whisper, his hard erection teasing my clit. "Please. All of you."

He traces light circles over one nipple then drags a hand down my side to hold my hip. "Are you begging for my cock, Reese?"

"Yes, I want it." *Forever.* "I want you to push inside me."

"To distract you?" he asks.

No, because I love you.

"Yes," I answer and keep my eyes shut so he can't read me.

He rocks into me, slowly and gently, and my soft sigh of pleasure fills the room. He sinks deep, and hot desire races through me. I move beneath him, my body tight and aching. He goes back on one elbow and his other hand spreads over my stomach, warming my skin, and filling me with erotic sensations. God, I love the familiar way he touches me, his tender lovemaking.

Lovemaking?

I never thought so before, but everything in his touch, in the way he looks at me, is so deeply caring that I can't help but wonder.

"This what you wanted, Reese?" he asks, his voice so deep I hardly recognize it. "To feel me like this? No barriers. Just you and me."

"Yes, it feels so good."

"Yeah, it fucking does." With a heavy breath, he lowers his head and captures my nipple. I swallow against the pleasure. His muscles flex as he powers into me, and I'm so lost in him I say, "Cole, I love…"

I pause, and my lids flash open as I catch myself.

"What do you love?" he asks, his deep-blue eyes drilling into me, and for a minute I fear he can see right into my soul. Then again, this is Cole, so maybe he can.

"I love this," I say quickly to cover my near slip, but when I see something in his eyes, something I thought I spotted that day we were cage diving, my heart misses a beat. Is it possible that he feels more, too? Do I dare hope that what we're doing here really is making love? Even if it is, though, how could we possibly make it work? We live on opposite sides of the country, and I'd never ask him to give up what he loves, or try to change him. Then again, I could move. Yeah, all my family and work are in New York. But Cole isn't. Who's to say he'd want me there, anyway? I pinch my eyes shut, my heart a confused mess.

He moves faster, penetrating deeper, creating a friction that has my inner muscles spasming and my thoughts spiraling out of control. Pleasure gathers and comes to a peak.

"I feel you," he whispers. "You're tightening around my cock, and it feels so fucking good, baby."

Every muscle in my body begins convulsing, as I shut my eyes and come all over his cock. My body trembles, shakes, and shudders as I moan in complete bliss.

"Fuuuck," he murmurs into my mouth. "You are so hot."

He slams into me, once, twice, then stills, spurting his hot cum high inside me. I squeeze around him, not wanting to lose a drop. He buries his face in my neck, his deep rhythmic breaths scorching my flesh as he pants. We both breathe together, cocooned against each other, and after a moment he lifts his head, his gaze meeting mine. One big hand goes to my hair, and he leans close, smoothing it from my forehead. Another soft kiss brushes my lips, warm, sensual...soul-stirring. My heart pounds so hard with the love I feel for him, I'm sure he can feel it.

"Did that work?" he asks, as his lips continue to brush gently over mine.

"Did what work?"

He grins. "Did all that kissing, and, you know, the sex and orgasms help distract you from the storm?"

"Storm?" is all I can manage to say, my post-orgasm brain still not working.

He laughs and falls into the bed beside me. "Guess so. We'll have to remember this game, Reesey Piecey."

Game?

Oh, right, I asked him to play a game with me. So, this *wasn't* lovemaking, after all.

It was just a sexy distraction.

Chapter Eight

COLE

Sitting in the cramped airplane as we approach the JFK runway, I steal a glance at Reese, and my heart squeezes so tight I can barely breathe.

She loves me.

I know her better than she knows herself, and I've been so goddamn caught up in my thoughts, so worried about losing her, that I haven't been thinking clearly. But what I realized last night as we lost ourselves in each other is that little Reesey Piecey fucking loves me.

She fucking loves me.

And now I finally get it. She's pushing me away on purpose. I love her for it. I really do. I love that she thinks she's doing what is best for me. But what she doesn't understand is just how much I love her, too, and nothing is more important to me than being with her, taking care of her, making her happy.

After she'd told me to leave, she said she didn't want to talk about it anymore. Fine, I won't talk about it, but I damn well plan to show her what she means to me, because no fucking way am I walking away from this without a fight. I plan to win, and the only way I'm going down is if she's beneath me.

During the long flight, I thought through everything that had happened over the last week, and the whole damn time I couldn't seem to wipe the stupid grin off my face. From the seat beside me, Reese kept casting curious glances my way. She probably thought I was excited about getting home so I could head back to Colorado. But this adventure, and me tagging along with her, had to be about getting the two of us together. Whoever set it up had to know how we felt about each other. Heck, I watched the shark dive video this morning when packing, and anyone who looks at us can surely see what we feel for each other. It's in the way we gaze at each other, in our body language.

I just need to figure out a way to show *her* how much I care, and how she is way more important to me than some job in Colorado, and that I really came home because I couldn't stay away for one more agonizing minute.

Can I make her believe that?

After we land, we exit the plane and make our way to our luggage. As we stand there waiting, Reese yawns and my phone pings. I rub my tired eyes and read the text from my brother, who's coming home next week for his high school reunion. Deciding to respond later, I shove my phone into my pocket, grab our luggage from the carousel, and follow Reese out into the dark night.

I hail a cab and climb in beside her. She's been so quiet, so out of sorts, that all I want to do is pull her into my arms and tell her everything will be all right. At least, I hope it will be. I hope the plan I've been mulling over will make everything right between us. If it doesn't, well… Nope. Stop. Not even going there. It has to work. Simple as that.

I give the cabbie Reese's address, and when he finally

pulls up to her condo, I open my door. She touches my hand to stop me.

"It's okay. I've got this."

"So do I."

"Cole, I can take care of myself," she says.

"I know you can. But if you think I'm letting you out on the sidewalk in the middle of the night, you don't know me at all. Now, come on. I am walking you to your door."

"Fine," she says. "Bossy much?" she adds under her breath.

I ignore the jibe because I know she's trying so hard to show me her independence so that I won't worry about her. I *do* know she can take care of herself. But goddammit, I want to take care of her. In fact, I want us to take care of each other, rely on each other, like two people who love each other should do.

I grab her luggage and follow her up the steps to her place. She unlocks the door and stands there for a second like she's not sure what to do next. Coming to her rescue, I drop a soft kiss onto the top of her head. "Night," I say.

She spins around. "Cole."

"Yeah?"

She goes quiet for a long time, shifting from one foot to the other. "Hate you."

I can't help but grin. "I know."

Chapter Nine

One long week has passed since we arrived home, and I've been going to work like a zombie and locking myself into my condo at night, wallowing in my own misery. Why did I think I could have sex with Cole and still be friends?

Stupid, stupid girl.

I look at my suitcase, which is still lying on the floor in the front entrance. I haven't even emptied it or washed the clothes that have Cole's scent on them. Oh, God, how could I have messed things up so badly?

Forcing myself up from the sofa and away from the ice cream that has become my best friend over the last week, I pad across the room and unzip the suitcase. The shark diving video falls out.

"How the heck did this get in my bag?"

Okay, great, now I'm talking to myself. I'm in worse shape than I thought. I shake my head and look at the disc. Maybe the laundry could wait. I walk over to the DVD, pop the disc in, and reach for my ice cream as I plunk back down on my comfy sofa.

When Cole comes into view, my heart races. I watch the way he takes care of me, holds me in his arms when the shark comes close. Yeah, and that's the reason I had to send him away. I'm not his responsibility, for God's sake. The man has a life to live, one that doesn't revolve around his chickenshit friend.

But when the camera zooms in on us, and I once again see something in Cole's eyes, something that resembles want and desire, my heart punches into my throat. I grab the remote and rewind to the beginning of the scene, sure I'm seeing things again. But no. There it is, caught on camera. In my heart, I can tell the way he is looking at me goes well beyond friendship. If I didn't know better, I'd say he was looking at me with love in his eyes. Not friendship love, but real love. The kind of love between two people who always put the other's best interests first.

Holy shit.

I drop the spoonful of ice cream and jump up, my pulse pounding so hard in my neck I think I might pass out. Just then my phone pings and I run to it. Please be Cole.

My heart sinks when I see the text from my friend Kennedy.

Hey, what's up?

My fingers fly over the screen.

Not much, you?

I'm in town to visit the family. Saw Cole at the airport.

Oh, God, he's leaving. He's really leaving. But why wouldn't he? I told him to go away and that I didn't want to discuss it anymore. Then again, why was he so damn happy on the plane? I thought it was because he was going to be heading back to Colorado soon. Now I just don't get it.

I mentally curse myself for being cruel. What if there really is more going on between us? I should have opened up, told him the truth. I can't let him go without doing that, without learning what he wants. I really should have told him how I felt, but I was too worried about our friendship, what was best for him. Maybe I had it all wrong.

I quickly text back.

Kennedy, I have to go.

Wait, you didn't tell me about your trip.

With time of the utmost importance, I can't give details, so I tell her, *we'll meet for coffee later.*

One thing, did you and Cole finally do it? :)

Oh. My. God.
What? I text back.

Come on, Reese. This is me. I know you. Why do you think I sent him on the trip with you?

You set the trip up?

Yeah, I picked your name.
I shake my head, hardly able to believe this.

And you sent Cole because you thought I wanted to 'do it' with him?

Uh, yeah! And he wants to do it with you, too, so I knew it was time for you two to get together. You did get together, right?

Yes, I text back and grab my purse. I have no idea what time his fight leaves—I'll check that in the cab—but right now I don't have a minute to waste.

I run to the front door, quickly lock it behind me, and race down the stairs so fast I nearly trip and land on my face. As I wobble and grab the rail to balance myself, a strong arm goes around my waist. I'm about to say thanks when I realize who's holding me.

"Where are you off to in such a hurry?"

"I…" I look past his shoulder and see a cab with the door still open. "I thought…"

Stormy blue eyes lock on mine. "You thought what?"

I choke back a big fat tear and burst out with, "I thought you'd left. Kennedy said she saw you at the airport."

He arches a brow, his grin playful. "And…you were coming after me?"

I point to my condo. "The video…I saw…Cole…" I put my arms around him and lay my cheek against this chest. I don't finish what I want to say because there is still some small part of me that isn't sure what he feels.

He holds me to him, and my heart fills with love as his powerful heart beats against my face. I take a moment to breathe in his scent and take comfort in his strength, in the way he's always been there to catch me. "I don't want to lose you," I say. "I don't want to wreck what we have between us. I couldn't handle it if we weren't friends anymore."

Or more…so much more.

"What makes you think you're going to lose me, or that you've wrecked things?"

"I told you to go away. That I didn't need you here."

"Yeah, and that's why we can't be friends anymore, Reese."

My heart misses a beat, and I try hard not to lose it in front of Cole. I nod like I totally understand and pull my face from his chest, doing my best not to cry.

He cups my chin and lifts it until we're eye to eye. "Reese," he says, "I thought *I'd* fucked everything up between us, but then I realized something very important."

"You did? What?"

"Come with me, and I'll show you." He guides me to the cab, and I slide in. He gives the cabbie directions to a place in Queens, and I just give him a strange look.

"You want to show me something in Queens?"

"You'll see," he says.

I mainly sit in quiet. We both do, as the driver takes us all the way to Queens. I want to open up to Cole, tell him everything, but I don't want to do it in front of the cabbie. A long while later, the cab stops in front of an older home—cute, but very run down.

"What are we doing here?" I ask.

Cole slides from the cab, and I follow him out. I glance up and down the street and see kids and dogs at a nearby park. "Do you know someone who lives here?"

"Yes."

Who?"

"Me," he answers.

My eyes go wide. "What are you talking about?"

"I bought this." He shrugs one shoulder. "Thought I could fix it up. Working construction with my uncle hasn't been so bad after all. I learned a few things."

I shake my head. This is all coming at me so fast. "Cole, that's amazing. But Colorado... I..."

He puts his hands on my shoulders and turns me. "See the garage?"

I nod.

"That would make a great clinic for you." I blink at him and try to process what he's saying. "There's lots of space in the backyard, too. We could build that shelter, Bed and

Barkfest." He glances up and down the street. "Outside the city, across from a park. Perfect location, don't you think? Took me all week to find it."

With my thoughts still two pages behind, I shake my head and ask, "Cole what are you saying?"

"Remember I said I realized something?"

"Yeah."

"Well, what I realized was that you love me."

"I do love you," I blurt out, unable to hold it in for one more second. "I didn't know how to tell you. I was so worried about losing you as a friend."

"I've loved you for a long time, but I didn't realize our friendship went so much deeper until our trip to Africa," he says, his voice low and soft. "I guess that's why I was so miserable when you were with Jared that I couldn't stay here, couldn't watch you two together."

"You…you love me?"

He laughs. "Fuck yeah, I love you. And that's why we can't go back to being just friends. When you told me to go away, it nearly killed me. But after making love to you that last night in the hotel, I realized what you were doing."

He loves me.

My heart soars as my entire body trembles with happiness. When I'm able to breathe again, I say, "Cole," as a tear falls down my cheek. I sniff, and he wipes it away.

"Hey, why are you crying?"

"I'm just…" My throat is so tight it's hard to get the words out. "I can't believe this is what you've been doing for the last week. When Kennedy said she saw you at the airport, I was so scared I'd lost you forever."

"I was at the airport because I had to pick up my brother. He's home for his upcoming high school reunion. I'll probably put him to work on the house while he's here.

At the mention of the house, I stiffen. Wait, I can't let Cole stay here, working in a job he hates. "What about Colorado and your work? You love it so much."

"Sure, it's great. It's a once in a lifetime adventure, and I've done it hundreds of times." He pulls me in tighter. "But the only adventure I want now is with you." He wags his finger between the two of us. "This is the once in a lifetime that I want, Reese. And it's time I started my own company."

"You always talked about that."

"I've been researching. Lots of opportunities for guides on the Hudson River."

I wriggle closer to him, and he drops a tender, slow, excruciatingly intimate kiss on my mouth. When he pulls back, I say, "What will you do in the off-season? There's not as much to do here as there is in Colorado. Will you be bored if you're not involved in some kind of adventure?"

"Bored? Hardly. And every day will be a new adventure taking care of our little ones."

I grin and nod toward the backyard where he wants to build Bed and Barkfest. "You mean our rescue dogs?"

His blue eyes soften as they race over my face. "No, Reese," he says, his thumb brushing my cheek so softly it turns me inside out. "I mean our kids. I want you to marry me. Have a family with me."

My heart misses a beat. *He wants to marry me. Have a family with me.* "Cole."

"Oh, and just so you know, I want a whole litter of little ones."

I laugh, and he laughs with me. "That's a lot of kids, Cole."

"Yup, and I'll be their stay-at-home daddy for the better part of the year." He dips his head, and his lips close over mine. His kiss is imbued with so much love I'm sure my heart is going to explode.

"Cole?"

He inches back and looks at me, his grin crooked. "What?

Still hate me?"

I laugh, everything between us so perfect that it's hard to explain what I'm feeling. Instead of trying, I say, "I love you."

His smile widens. "Yeah, I know, and it's damn well time you told me that!"

I whack him and can't help but laugh. "God, I hate you."

He laughs with me. "Hate you, too."

Acknowledgments

To the amazing team at Entangled, who do so much work behind the scenes, thank you!

About the Author

New York Times and *USA Today* bestselling author Cathryn Fox is a wife, mom, sister, daughter, and friend. She loves dogs, sunny weather, anything chocolate (she never says no to a brownie), pizza, and red wine. Cathryn has two teenagers who keep her busy and a husband who is convinced he can turn her into a mixed martial arts fan. When not writing, Cathryn can be found laughing over lunch with friends, hanging out with her kids, or watching a big action flick with her husband.

WICKED TAKEOVER
a *Wicked Brand* novel by Tina Donahue

Not only has Lauren lost her corporate job, but she's just inherited a struggling West Palm Beach tattoo parlor...along with the virile due who runs it. Dante's sinfully hot with a killer smile and beautifully inked biceps, and Lauren wants him badly. Recognizing the sexy woman beneath the conservative suit, Dante encourages her to loosen up and have some wicked fun. Until lust turns to surprising need and friendship to something deeper.

SEDUCING HIS TRUE LOVE
a *Small Town Temptations* novel by Laura Jardine

Blaine Richards didn't believe in love at first sight, even when he met the perfect woman. They had an intense, passionate interlude sixteen months ago...and then it was over. Even after all this time, Blaine can't forget Cassie Monroe. He challenges her to spend a weekend with him, betting she won't be able to walk away at the end. Cassie finally agrees, determined to prove there's nothing between them but hot sex.

PAYBACK
a *Viking Bastards* novel by Christina Phillips

I don't fuck girls who work for me, but as soon as Amelia turns those big green eyes on me I know she's trouble. I can't keep my hands off her, and the *almost-but-not-quite-sex* we share in the kitchen is the hottest thing I've ever had. Except she calls it quits, before we've even started. She's all I can think about. Until I find out who she is and what she really wants. She's after payback, but there's no way she's going to get it. No way in hell…

UNTAMED
Part One of the *Uninhibited!* serial by Lauren Hawkeye

Celebrity archaeologist Cari Dunn is so over Georgia, with its heat, red-tape, and the slew of threatening messages painted on her motel door. She just wants to dig, the network wants to keep her safe—with Jasper Benjamin, a bodyguard that radiates raw masculinity. Just looking at him penetrates her to the core and ignites passion she's never felt. Sleeping with her bodyguard is easy. Staying alive is harder.

Made in United States
Cleveland, OH
08 May 2025

16773960R00059